DON'T MENTION THE HEN WEEKEND

A MARY BROWN NOVEL

BERNICE BLOOM

Bernice Bloom

CHAPTER 1

'OK my lovely, I'm going to blindfold you,' says Ted.

I look at him cautiously. 'Why on earth do you want to do that?'

'Stop asking questions and do as you are told.'

He's being terribly assertive. Not like Ted at all. He takes my bag off my shoulders and shuffles me to the side of the hallway.

'What is going on?'

'No questions,' he repeats, like some mafia boss.

It's 6 pm, and I've just arrived back from work in the stifling heat, to find my boyfriend Ted behaving like Al Pacino while dressed like James Bond. He's got a tuxedo on, and he's polished his shoes. He's even wearing aftershave, for heaven's sake. And he's been off work today. He rarely gets out of his pyjamas on a day off, let alone showering and dressing like he's off to a film premiere. This is odd.

Then he holds up the blindfold again, and 'odd' doesn't seem a strong enough word.

'This is going on your eyes whether you like it or not.'

'Look, Ted, I'd really like to know what's happening. And where's Elvis?'

Elvis is my new puppy. He usually jumps up and down like he's on a trampoline when I arrive home in the evenings, but there's no sign of him tonight.

'Elvis is fine. Sarah has taken him for a walk. They'll be back in an hour.'

'And what's that smell?'

A delicious aroma wafts through from the kitchen, mingling with the smell of aftershave to create an intoxicating and rather alluring combination.

'Have you got us a takeaway?'

'Nope.'

'Yes, you have. I can smell it.'

'I've been cooking. Now keep still so I can put this on you.'

He's been cooking? Frankly, that's odder than him trying to blindfold me. I didn't think he knew where the kitchen was.

Ted leads me into the dining room. It's quite a painful experience, to be honest. I mean - I don't want to seem ungrateful when he's put so much work into this surprise, but he's not a good leader, and by the time he gets me to the dining chair, I'm bruised from bashing into the doorframe and every piece of furniture en route to my seat.

'OK, safely there. Now sit still.'

Ted leaves the room, and I'm dying to tear off the blindfold and check for bruises, but that's not really in the spirit of things, is it? So instead, I sit quietly while lights flicker in front of me, visible through the material around my eyes. There are obviously candles on the table, but I can't see much else.

An air of mystery pervades.

The door squeaks as it opens, and I hear Ted come in and

lay something down heavily on the table. Then there's a scraping of crockery as he takes the lid off the pot, and a lovely smell lifts into the air. It smells like a Viennese bistro. He leaves the room again and returns with what sounds like more pots. Then there's the sound of wine being poured. Excellent: like music to my ears.

'OK, are you ready?' he asks, moving behind me. 'Here's a surprise for you.'

He removes the blindfold, and I'm so shocked at the sight that greets me that a strange sound escapes from somewhere near the back of my throat.

'Ted, this is stunning,' I say. I reach over to touch him lightly on the arm.

The room is filled with candles, shimmering and shining in the early evening light. Ted has put fans in the room to keep us cool, making the candle flames flicker and dance even more.

'I'm glad you like it,' he says in an unusually deep voice. If this is some sort of seduction routine, it's working. Though it's rather unnecessary...I'm so in love with Ted and fancy him so much that all he's got to do is look at me, and I'm his.

'I can't believe you've done all this.'

'Wait till you taste the food,' he says. 'I found the recipe online after you said you loved the Italian meal we had the other day. Do you remember - at Sposami?'

'Oh, I don't, but I'm sure it will be lovely. It smells delicious.'

He kisses me lightly on the cheek and serves me a portion of this gorgeous chicken casserole. There's a side salad and great big chunks of garlic bread, so pungent with the smell of fresh garlic that I know I'll be smelling of it for weeks. The bread is dripping with butter. Honestly, it's like being in heaven.

'I don't think I've ever tasted anything so utterly delicious,' I say. And I really mean it. Even if the food had been terrible, I'd have told Ted that it was nice, just to encourage him, but this is properly gorgeous.

'I don't remember ever going to an Italian restaurant where the food was this good,' I say. 'I really mean that, Ted. This is wonderful. Thank you.'

Ted fills my glass and sits back in his chair.

'You don't remember Sposami?'

'Gosh, it's so odd, but I really don't. And if the food had been this good, I know I'd have remembered it.'

'Why don't you look up Sposami?' he suggests.

I take a sip and look around at the candles flickering.

'Look it up,' he says again, pushing his phone towards me. 'That'll help you to remember it.'

I take his phone and look up the details for the restaurant as Ted stands up and moves around the table to join me.

S-p-o-s-a-m-i I type into the phone.

'Oh my God.'

There on the phone is the translation of the Italian word. It's not a restaurant; it says 'Marry Me.' I feel myself beaming like a lunatic, my cheeks reddening as I sit there looking at him, almost crying with delight.

Ted has dropped to one knee and is holding out a ring box with a beautiful diamond engagement ring nestling inside.

'Well, will you?'

'YES!' I say. 'A hundred times YES.'

My God, life is wonderful. Isn't it? Isn't it just bloody marvellous? I can't believe this. He sits back down and watches as I move the eternity ring he gave me six months ago onto the other hand, so he can slip the new ring onto my finger. Our legs are touching, and I want them always to be next to each other. I want to be close to him forever. Then he wraps me up in a huge hug.

'We're engaged,' he whispers into my ear. 'You and me, girl. We're gonna spend the rest of our lives together.'

We stay there, wrapped in the moment, for what feels like ages. Then, I start crying on Ted's shoulder as he tells me everything he loves about me. My humour, my silliness, my kindness, the chaos surrounding me. All the things I think are a bit wrong with me - he loves them.

'There's something I'd really like to do,' he says.

'Oh yeah. I bet there is.'

'No - not that. Well, yes - I'd like to do that. I'd definitely like to do that, but there's something that would make me happy concerning our wedding.'

Just hearing him say the 'w' word and my stomach makes a little loop and feels full of butterflies. I'm getting married. Ted and me. Husband and wife.

'What would make you happy?'

'I'd like us to get married quickly. You know how some couples spend years planning the wedding, then fall out over the colour of the placemats and whether Aunty Hilda should sit next to Bob, the office predator. All that rubbish about bridesmaids' dresses and matching veils and shoes? I want you to have the wedding of your dreams, but I don't want to wait forever to marry you. And I want this to be about us... you and me.'

'OK,' I reply. 'Well, that sounds perfectly reasonable. So let's do that.'

'Great. Let's get married on 1st September.'

'Wow, that's really soon.'

'I know.'

'Is it possible to organise a wedding so quickly?'

The doorbell rings, indicating the return of Elvis, and Ted goes to answer the door. 'Just think about it,' he says as he leaves the room.

I pick up Ted's phone, still lying on the dining table with

the English translation of Sposami written on it, and I look to see what the date is today. It's 1st August. A month. Can we organise a wedding in a month? Also, 1st September is a Tuesday. Is it sensible to get married on a Tuesday?

Elvis comes racing into the room and jumps up, demanding attention, as I lay Ted's phone back down. A month? Would we get a venue?

'What do you think?' asks Ted.

'I love the idea of doing it quickly, but I don't know how far in advance you have to order flowers, dresses, and things like that.'

'If we can't get them in time, we don't have them.'

'But I want lots of flowers.'

'Then we tell everyone to bring a bouquet to the church with them.'

'I guess.'

'I think we can make this wedding simple, gorgeous, and full of love. Let's not make it a huge nightmare like when my sister married. She almost split up from her husband-to-be with the amount of drama that ensued.'

That's undoubtedly true. It was the most stressful time ever. So I know what Ted means, and I agree that it would be great not to make a huge drama out of the whole thing. But… a month? Really?

CHAPTER 2

We move into the sitting room for dessert. I'd love to tell you that we moved because it was a more romantic place in which to sit, but the truth is that Elvis pooed on the floor, and the smell was disgusting…quite overwhelming. So I left Ted to clear it up and escaped to the sitting room where I am now lying on the sofa next to the fan, with a rather sheepish-looking puppy by my side.

Ted comes in carrying the wine and a gorgeous chocolate mousse, laced with caramel and full of toffee pieces. He puts it down and turns away for a moment, allowing me the opportunity to stick my finger into it at the edge and sweep up the lovely, sweet chocolatey taste. My God, it's good. I could eat the whole lot. Which I almost do, to be fair. I devour the large portion that Ted serves, run my fingers around the edge of my bowl to ensure I've got every last smear of caramel-infused loveliness, and lick each of my fingers like a four-year-old.

'I feel like I should ring people and tell them our news,' I say, settling back into the sofa.

'Not tonight. Let's keep it our secret and let the world in

tomorrow.'

'You're quite romantic sometimes, Ted. I never realised when we first met, but you have a huge soppy side.'

'Don't tell anyone,' he says, leaning over to kiss me gently on my cheek. Then we both switch off our phones and wallow in the loveliness of it all...our engagement is a warm secret nestling between the two of us as we lie there, wrapped in a cocoon of love on that warm summer's evening.

We fall asleep like that; Ted, Elvis, the ring, and me, and it's lovely. Until I wake up with achy shoulders and a creaky neck and look up to see Ted dangling over the edge of the sofa with his glasses askew and Elvis draped around his neck. It's 4am.

'Bed?'

'Sure, just as soon as I've removed my puppy scarf.'

We trudge to the bedroom in a trance-like state and collapse into bed without talking, then I hear Ted whisper. 'You're going to be my wife,' and the wave of loveliness that coloured the evening sweeps me up over me again.

Ted has to get up and go to work the following day, whereas I have the morning off. I hear the door shut as he leaves at 7am, and by 7.01am, I'm on the phone with Charlie to regale her with the details of the feast we had the night before. I tell her about the delicious casserole and the chocolatey pudding.

'You won't believe what happened then,' I say.

'Go on...'

'He proposed.'

There is a scream that almost shatters my phone, then silence.

'It's a good thing,' I say.

'I know, I know. I'm so pleased for you, I can't find the words...this is just awesome. Why didn't you tell me that immediately instead of jabbering on about the chicken and the wine?'

'I wanted to build up the tension. And you know what's also great?'

'What?'

'We've decided not to have a long engagement but to get married quickly.'

'What? Next summer?'

'No, sooner than that. We're getting married in a month.'

Another silence.

'Charlie, why do you keep going quiet?'

'Well, a month. That's so soon. I mean - how will you get everything done?'

'If we can't get it done, we won't do it.'

'I don't think you'll be able to get a wedding dress that quickly. And can you book venues and things? You can't get married down the pub in leggings and your horrible Mickey Mouse t-shirt.'

'Hopefully, it won't come to that, but I'll need your help, or nothing will happen. I'm off tomorrow; fancy brunch to start planning?'

'I think we better meet for breakfast instead; we'll need all morning. I'll start assembling information for us to discuss. I'll get some wedding magazines and things like that. Do you have any idea what sort of wedding you want?'

'Not at all.'

'Have you thought about how many people you want?'

'Nope.'

'Have you thought about whether you want a church wedding?'

'Nope.'

'Have you thought about whether you want to do something local?'

'Nope.'

'OK, well - that's loads for me to go on, then. Thanks, Mary. I'll start thinking.'

'Thanks, mate.'

Five minutes later, Charlie calls back.

'Do you want a hen night?' she asks.

'Oh yes. Definitely yes,' I reply.

'Good. I was dreading you answering 'nope' to that question too. OK, so I'll get a list of everything we need to do, and we'll talk in the morning.'

'Thanks, angel.'

'I'm so pleased for you, Mary. It's great news.'

'I know, Charlie. I can't quite believe it. It's the best thing ever. And he did it so well…the food, the wine, him being so attentive. The whole thing with the name of the Italian restaurant not being an Italian restaurant at all... It was perfect. Well, until Ted pooed all over the floor. That wasn't so wonderful.'

'Ted pooed on the floor? What?'

'Yes - I had to go into the other room because it smelled so disgusting, but it was still really romantic.'

'Was it?'

'Yes, of course it was! I'm getting married to the man I love. We're going to be together forever and ever…what could be more romantic?'

'Not shitting on the floor would be good. Did he just get excited or something? It seems so odd. I can't imagine him doing that.'

'He's quite good, most of the time, but he does it occasionally.'

'He's done this before?'

'Not frequently, but he does it from time to time. It was strange last night because he'd just come in from a walk. Usually, he does it outside, on his walk.'

'Oh, hang on. You mean Elvis pooed on the floor.'

'Yes. That's what I said.'

'No - you said Ted. You definitely said Ted.'

'What? You thought Ted had pooed on the floor after asking me to marry him?'

'I thought it was odd, but - yes. That's what you said.'

'I need to stop confusing the names. I told the guys at work yesterday that Elvis had given me a lift in.'

'Yes, you need to stop doing that. You told me a few weeks ago that you would give Ted a bath because he was getting matted around his bum.'

'Yeah, that wasn't my finest moment.'

Having cleared up the situation and reassured my friend about the state of my husband-to-be's bowels, it was time to go to work. I planned to ring Juan from the bus, tell him about the engagement and invite him to join us the following morning. If I left it to Charlie, he'd get all upset about me preferring her and not sparing the time to tell him myself. Juan can be sensitive like that.

Then there's the whole situation with our parents...Ted and I decided last night that we should go and visit both sets of parents tonight to tell them the good news. We want them to hear from us, in the flesh, so we can raise a glass of champagne and celebrate with them. But now I'm worried. Perhaps I should just phone mum and tell her, in case she hears from someone else? She'd hate it if someone else told her.

I sit for a while as the bus rumbles along, stopping to pick up people who look so familiar to me. I see them every day. I want to scream out to them that I got engaged last night. I'm dying to talk to people about it.

It's no good. I'm going to have to tell mum. I won't be able to keep quiet about it all day. So I'll phone her and give her the news but make her promise to say she doesn't know when Ted and I turn up this evening.

What could go wrong with that plan?

Alas, quite a lot.

'Say that again,' she says after I tell her about the proposal, but that she must not mention to anyone that I'm getting married, and she needs to pretend that she knows nothing about it when we arrive this evening.

'It's quite straightforward, mum.'

'No, it's not. I'm not sure why you're pretending to get married to Ted,' she says.

'No, we're not pretending. We *are* getting married. But I need you to pretend you don't know.'

'Oh, I see. Well, it's wonderful that you're getting married. I'm so pleased. Let me get your father so you can tell him.'

'No. This is the thing - I know I'm being a pain, but Ted and I have decided to come and tell you together this evening, but I couldn't wait that long to talk to you - so I'm telling you now. But could you pretend you don't know when we come tonight, so Ted doesn't know I've told you? And don't mention it to dad, so he looks surprised.'

'OK,' she says, without sounding convinced about this.

'Thanks, mum. Don't mention it to anyone. We'll see you later and tell you properly, including all the details.'

THERE IS a lovely positive reaction at work, as people I've been working with for almost 10 years hug me and tell me that Ted is a fortunate man. Even Keith, my boss, is astonishingly kind to me. All quite disconcerting, really.

'What did your mum say?' asks Karren. She's my favourite person at work. She's the only one of them whom I socialise with.

'We're going to tell both parents tonight,' I say. 'I'm sure they'll be delighted; they love Ted.'

'I bet they do...Ted's really lovely.'

'Well, I, for one, am very pleased for you,' says Keith. 'I'm sure your mum will be thrilled. I'm fond of Ted. He's the sort of man I think you should marry.'

'Thank you,' I reply, though I'm not sure what he's talking about. What 'sort of man' is Ted? And what 'sort' of person does that make me?

So many questions. But Keith has moved on.

'As a wedding gift, we'd like to provide the flowers for the big day and for your bridal bouquet,' he says. 'Anything you want - just say, and the company will provide them for you. All free of charge.'

'Oh, wonderful. Thank you, Keith. That's a lovely present. I can just picture the church full of lilies and orchids. Roses cascading down the pillars.'

'Yeah, don't go mad, Mary, will you?'

'No, of course not. Do you want to give me a budget or something?'

'That's the last thing I want to do. I'm not going to limit what you can have on your wedding day. Have anything you want. Just be reasonable. Daffodils are every bit as lovely as orchids. And...word to the wise, Mary. Marriage can be difficult.'

'OK, Keith. Thanks. That's very helpful. And very kind - the flowers. I'll think about the whole thing and come back to you.'

'Yep, you do that.'

He walks away, muttering about how the most expensive things are not always the best, and I turn back to the task at hand...getting the till points decorated with the new flowers that have come into the store. You wouldn't believe how much people buy at till points when they've got their trolley in front of them, they'll throw in some flowers as if they're free.

'The banners go up first,' I say to Barbara, who is

supposed to be helping me today but is spending most of her time watching the attractive new guy in the maintenance department.

'His trousers are too tight,' she says. 'Not complaining, but look at the way they have to stretch when he bends over.'

'Yeah, you're sounding like a pervert now, Barbara. Can you pass me the cardboard cut-out that the roses go into?'

She passes the container, and I stand it on the back of the till unit.

'I don't think I'd like to get married like you are.'

'Really? Why not?'

'Mary, don't take this the wrong way, but it feels like settling. I mean, Ted's nice - I don't mean there's anything wrong with Ted, just that the world is full of amazing men. What if a better one comes along?'

'I guess you don't get married until you've met someone you think is perfect for you.'

'So, if a man comes along tomorrow who is just as lovely as Ted but earns a fortune and is a Prince of some beautiful Caribbean Island, you wouldn't be tempted?'

'No.'

'What even if you got on better with him than with Ted?'

'Yeah, but I wouldn't. Ted and I are perfect together.'

'But just say you did. You'd regret it then, wouldn't you? Especially since he'd fly you on his private jet to his private island.'

'I don't think that's going to happen. I'm happy with Ted.'

'Yeah, but what if...'

'No, Barbara. I'm happy with Ted.'

'You have to admit that it's interesting.'

She's playing hard and loose with the word 'interesting' there. 'Pass me the wire cutters, Barbara.'

CHAPTER 3

'Come on then, my little daffodil,' says Ted. He calls me that whenever I wear this yellow linen jacket. He says it to be kind, but the truth is that I don't look like a daffodil; I resemble nothing so much as Laa-Laa from the Teletubbies. You know - the one who likes to party all the time (how do I know this stuff? I watch too much tv).

I have to wear this hideous jacket tonight because Ted's mum bought it for me, and she loves it when I wear it.

To make it all so much worse, I'm wearing yellow lace gloves with the jacket (if you're going to look ridiculous, you might as well look *really* absurd), and the plan is for me to rip them off and reveal the ring. Then, I'll have to put them back on when we go to Ted's and do the whole ripping them off thing again.

'Hello darling,' says mum, answering the door. 'What in the name of the lord are you wearing?'

'Oh look, it's Bart Simpson,' says dad.

'Oh ha, ha. You two are so amusing.' I kick off my shoes in the porch and throw my jacket into the cloakroom. Then I hurl myself into the small armchair in the corner of the sitting room, the one I always loved so much when I was young. Something about being at home sends me reeling back through time. Suddenly I'm like a teenager again, dangling my legs over the edge of the armrest. I'll demand they put on Top of the Pops in a minute.

'So...here we all are then. When are you going to tell us?' asks mum.

Ted looks at me and tips his head to the side in a way that says, *I'm very disappointed in you*. I look at my feet, hanging off the edge of the sofa, and interrogate the chipped red polish that desperately needs removal.

'We'll all have a chat soon,' I say.

'Well, let me go and make some tea then,' she says, scurrying off to the kitchen. But no sooner have we heard her fill up the kettle with water than there's a loud knock at the door.

'Oh damn,' shouts mum. 'That will be the window cleaner. I meant to hide, but he's bound to have heard us. Damn. I usually pretend to be out.'

'Mum!' I say. 'You can't do that. You have to pay him if he's cleaned your windows. The poor man's got to make a living.'

'I know, dear. I know. But it always seems very imposing when he's knocking on the door, and I never have the right money.'

'I've got some cash on me,' says Ted, pushing his hands into his pockets.

'No, silly, Don't worry - I've got a little stash in the kitchen.'

'If you've got a little stash in the kitchen, why on earth are you trying not to pay him.'

'I don't know, really. I never want to pay for the window cleaner. Doesn't everyone hide?'

I'm just about to tell her that - no, people don't hide from window cleaners when she opens the door, and it's not a payment-seeking window cleaner, but Aunty Susan and Uncle Mark. They are accompanied by mum's neighbours Barry, Sandra, and their odd son Malcolm.

Uncle Mark is carrying a cake, Aunty Susan is blowing a party horn, and the others all have balloons. They are smiling and skipping as they come into the room. 'Congratulations!' they shout when they see Ted and me. 'We're so pleased for you both.'

They then burst into a chorus of 'Mary's getting married in the morning...' followed swiftly by 'Here comes the bride....'

What they lack in melody, they make up for with volume.

I daren't look at Ted.

When the music eventually stops, mum looks over at us sheepishly.

'Come with me, Susan; I'm just putting the kettle on.'

Mum goes into the kitchen to make the tea, and I hear her telling off Susan in one of those whispers so loud that she might as well be speaking in her normal voice.

'Sorry,' says Susan. 'But why does it have to be a secret? They're a wonderful couple. I know how much you love Ted. This is an evening for joy and celebration.'

'They just wanted it to be a secret until they told me.'

'But I thought Mary already told you?'

'Yes, she did, but...oh, it's complicated. They wanted it to be a secret until they told me formally.'

Ted stands up and walks into the kitchen.

'Come here, ladies,' he says. 'I need to hug my mother-in-law and aunty-in-law to be.'

There's a couple of minutes of silence when I assume the hugging is taking place before I hear Aunty Susan's voice: 'I'm very sorry if I did something wrong.'

'You did nothing wrong. We thought it would be nice to

tell you all face-to-face, but Mary wanted to tell you straight away, and I don't blame her. This cake looks delicious, by the way. And I have some champagne here, shall we open that instead of messing around with tea?'

'Good idea,' says mum.

I hear glasses being removed from cupboards and plates being taken out of the dishwasher. I stay still, sitting on the sofa, with my legs dangling over the edge.

'Everything OK?' asks dad.

'Yes, really good.'

'Work going OK?'

'Yes.'

'I'm glad about that,' he says, leaning back in his chair.

Dad's hopeless at talking about anything emotional, but - even for him - that's a bit crazy.

'Did you hear that Ted and I are getting married?' I say. 'I think that's what they're all chatting about in the kitchen.'

'Yes, that's rather good news, isn't it?'

'What's going on in here?' asks mum. Ted walks behind her, gallantly carrying the tray with cake, plates, and glasses. Aunty Susan is walking just behind him, holding the bottle of champagne.

'Dad was just asking about work.'

'Jolly good. Have you got a rash on your hands or something?'

'No, I'm fine.'

'Why are you wearing gloves in this heat? Do you need some cream for them? You used to get terrible eczema on them when you were a gymnast.' Then she turns to my dad: 'Go and get the cream from the bathroom, would you, love.'

Dad stands up to do what's asked of him while I try to reassure mum that I'm not in the least troubled by a skin complaint and we'd like everyone to sit down and enjoy cake and champagne.

'I'm fine, honestly,' I say.

'What? You're going to eat cake with gloves on, are you?'

'No - I'm going to take the gloves off as soon as everyone sits down.'

Ted puts his arm around me as I take off my gloves.

'Look,' I say, revealing the diamond sparkling on my finger.

There's a gasp from Mum, and she falls back a little so that she's almost sitting on Uncle Mark's lap. Aunty Susan blows on the party horn, and dad returns to the room with an assortment of unwanted skin creams.

'Oh, that ring is wonderful,' says mum. 'That's wonderful. We're so pleased for you.'

Even Dad looks moved. He puts down his medicinal creams and walks over to Ted, and the two men shake hands. 'I promise to look after her,' says Ted. 'She's in safe hands.'

Mum hugs me and tells me it's the best news she's ever heard.

Once Ted and dad have stopped their manly bonding routine, dad hugs me too, telling me that Ted is a fortunate man, but I am very lucky too, and he couldn't wish for anyone better for me to marry.

It's like he's a different person from five minutes ago. I think he just doesn't know how to react to happy news. Ike many men of his generation, he's been encouraged to offer a stiff upper lip in times of emotion. But now he can see everyone hugging, so he follows suit. I can see he's genuinely happy by the news as he smiles warmly and even looks like he's about to cry.

'Thank you both so much,' says Ted. 'Mary and I are excited about it and can't wait to spend the rest of our lives together.'

Mum wants to know all the details about the proposal, of course, and she clasps her hands to her chest as I tell her about the beautiful meal and the joke about the Italian restaurant which turned out to be 'marry me' in Italian.

'Oh, you are a romantic,' she says, grabbing Ted for another hug. Mum is quite slight, certainly slimmer than I am, and she looks like a tiny delicate doll in Ted's massive arms. I feel a wave of love for the man I'm going to marry. And a surge of emotion for the parents who have given me the strength to go out there and meet a man like Ted.

'Have you started to think about the wedding?' says mum. 'I don't suppose you've had time, but things get booked up quite quickly when it comes to weddings, and everything takes forever to come.

'Janine's daughter got married recently and had to wait four months for the wedding dress to be ready. She booked the hall for the reception about a year in advance. Honestly, it's crazy. Once you're ready to think about it, let's make some plans.'

'We have decided we'd like to do it quite soon because neither of us wants years of preparation and grief. So we're going to get on with it.'

'How lovely,' says mum. 'Perhaps a lovely garden wedding next summer? Or maybe that's a bit too soon?'

'We were thinking of doing it even sooner than that. We want to get married in a month.'

'A month?'

Mum looks over at dad, who shrugs because he doesn't know the first thing about wedding planning and has no idea what response the news of a tight timetable demands.

'I know it's very soon, but we've decided to do it, and anything that can't be planned in a month, we won't have.'

'It sounds like a bloody good idea,' says Dad. 'All this grief and pain involved in planning weddings is ridiculous. The two of you love each other, and the wedding is just a small part of marriage. So let's organise the best wedding we can as quickly as possible.'

'Thanks, dad,' I say, leaning over to touch his shoulder. I know he'll be embarrassed if I jump up and hug him. He's probably all hugged out. So I confine myself to that small gesture. Mum and Aunty Susan look on in bafflement. Dad has stepped in with an opinion on the wedding plans. No one expected that.

'Well, let's think about it, shall we?' says mum.

'I'm going to meet Charlie for breakfast, and we'll put together a list of everything we need to do. Then I'll call you, and we'll make plans.'

'Right,' she says. 'OK, do that.'

'I can't believe how well that went,' I say to Ted as I slip into my lemon-coloured jacket, despite the heat, and slip my hands into the yellow gloves. 'They seemed supportive.'

'Yes, they did. I'm very fond of your mum and dad. But, of course, they did have the considerable advantage of knowing in advance that we were getting married.'

'Ah, yes. Sorry about that. I was worried that someone would tell mum before I could. I thought I could mention it on the phone, and she'd keep quiet.'

'Yeah - like that was ever going to happen.'

'I know. I'm sorry.'

Ted hugs me and kisses me lightly on the top of my head. 'Don't worry. It's not a problem at all. I hope my parents are the same. Dad can be a bit awkward at times.'

I glance at Ted as he says this. He might just have made the understatement of the year. Ted's dad can be utterly miserable when he wants to be. He is the opposite of Ted; while Ted is encouraging and eager to look on the bright side, his dad likes to sit in his favourite armchair, predicting doom and gloom. His mum is lovely, but it always feels like he overshadows her. She runs around making tea and looking after everyone while he sits there. And I know a lot of people's parents are like that. My mum does all the work around the house and ensures everyone is OK when we have guests, but dad will do the hoovering and tidying up when people are gone. I can't imagine Ted's dad ever doing anything.

We arrive at their little cottage and are led straight into the front room, which is so hot I fear my skin will melt. The television is blaring out like we're in an old people's home with no fans or open windows. The place is at boiling point. I instantly regret wearing the jacket. I only wore it because she bought it for me, but she hasn't noticed. I feel like a bloody lemon. And I look like one, too, for Christ's sake. I slip it off but leave the gloves on. Now I look like I'm in a terrible Michael Jackson tribute band or something.

'Have a seat, love,' she says, and I sit down next to Ted's dad, who is reclining in his ancient armchair, which rocks a bit when it moves and gives this loud creak that reminds me of old men in those all-American mid-west films, out on the 'stoop,' chewing a piece of hay and contemplating the world.

The only difference is that the guys in the films impart words of wisdom and common-sense borne of a lifetime's adventure. Ted's dad just radiates sadness and disappointment. He looks like his dog just died or someone reversed over his foot. And he farts a lot. Sorry to share all the gruesome details, but he really does. I've never known anyone to emit such ripe smells all the time.

'So, we have some great news to tell you,' says Ted.

'How exciting,' says his mum, enthusiastically wiping her hands on her apron.

'We're getting married.'

'Oh, how wonderful.' His mum clasps her hands to her face in joy and delight. 'That's fantastic. I'm so pleased. So very pleased.'

Ted's dad is silent.

'Did you hear that, dad? We're getting married.'

'Jolly good,' he says.

'Come here,' says Ted's mum, holding out her arms. 'Give me a big hug. You're going to be my daughter-in-law. I couldn't be happier.'

I look around at Ted's dad. He's smiling. I can't believe it. He doesn't get up to hug me, but he reaches out to touch my hand, which means a lot. He's never shown me the slightest warmth before.

'I don't think I've ever been so happy,' I say to them both. 'I promise to be the best wife in the world.'

CHAPTER 4

'You know there's a hell of a lot to do, don't you?' says Charlie before I've even had the chance to sit down.

'Yes, but we can do it.'

I'm buoyed by the successful trips to Ted and my parents and feel like nothing is impossible. I pull out a notebook to show her how committed I am and turn to the first page with a flourish.

'I've thought about the questions you were asking me yesterday, and now I have all the answers so we can start planning. Mum is up for helping us, Juan is obviously available to help, and we have loads of friends. So, where do we start?'

'Good, right. If you're committed to this, we need to start by understanding what wedding you want. What are you thinking?'

'I want a small wedding. Just a get-together of our families and the close friends who matter. Only a dozen or so people. I don't want to make it unwieldy, and I don't want to invite every person I've ever met. I want this to mean something."

'OK, well, that's a good start.'

The waiter walks past, and we both order cappuccinos.

'If you genuinely only want a dozen people, then it should be manageable, but that's not very many. So who do you want to come from your side of the family?'

'I suppose just mum, dad, Aunty Susan, and Uncle Mark. That's all.'

'And what about Ted's family?'

'Well, he's got his mum and dad, his sister and her husband.'

'That's eight. You're sure there aren't any rogue aunts or uncles knocking around or cousins that need to be invited?'

'I'll check with Ted, but I don't think so. We're both from quite small families. I've not met any other relatives. So a dozen people should be fine.'

'But you haven't added any friends yet.'

'I'd like, say, six friends.'

'And Ted?'

'Probably the same.'

'Right, so 20 of the 12 places are filled already.'

'Oh lord. Yes, good point. Maybe a dozen is too few. Let's say 20.'

'Shall we say 30 maximum? To be safe.'

'Yes. That'll be more than enough.'

'And you're sure Ted doesn't want a huge wedding or anything like that? His mum's not expecting to invite all her friends from the bridge club or the choir?'

'No. I mean - I don't think so. Ted was the one who came up with the idea of doing this quickly, so he's going to have to tell her no. He keeps saying, 'if it can't be organised in time, we won't have it. Let's keep the wedding simple,' so that's what we're doing.'

'Yes, you're right - he will have to talk to his mum to avoid conflicts later. Make sure you remind him, won't you? If he wants a hundred people at this thing, it can't be organised in a month.'

My cappuccino comes, and I send the waiter back for a pain au chocolat. This is altogether more stressful than I thought it would be.

'I printed out all these notes from the internet,' says Charlie, taking crumpled pieces of paper out of her bag. 'It's a list of everything you need to do to plan a wedding.'

'But it's about eight pages long, and why's it all screwed up?'

'I know it's long; that's because there's a lot to do. All the websites I went onto suggested that we should plan a minimum of a year before the event. I thought that was ridiculous, so I screwed the pages up and printed off another list, but that suggested you needed a minimum of 18 months, so I pulled this first one out of the bin and flattened it out. That's why it's still a bit creased.'

I look at the list with hundreds of things on it, and I scan until my eye catches 'one month to go.' It says: 'by now, you should be all planned and ready to relax before the wedding.'

'So, I'm a year behind before we've even started?'

'That's about the size of it,' says Charlie, as Juan opens the door with such force that it rattles, forcing everyone to spin around and look. Or it could be his outfit that is causing the stares. He comes tripping through the door in cherry red cowboy boots, ripped jeans, and a skin-tight black vest. He offers a jaunty wave as he heads over.

'How's it going?'

'Not wonderfully. This is the bloody list of how to plan a wedding. It suggests that by one month to go, everything should be done. We haven't even started.'

Juan kisses me on the cheek. 'Don't worry, lovely. We will

get cracking. Everything's going to be fine. Your wedding will be better than any wedding these people could ever create.'

'Thank you, there's just so much to do.'

'And stressing about it is not going to help at all. Take a look at my new boots if you need something to cheer you up. I feel like an urban cowboy in these.'

We look down at Juan's feet. Neither of us says a word. I think I speak for us both when I say they are the ugliest boots we have ever seen. Truly awful.

'Let me update you on the plans so far,' says Charlie. 'Mary has agreed to limit the number of guests at the wedding to 30 people.'

'Yep.'

'Well, that's as far as we've got.'

'What? That's all the planning you've done?'

'That's it.'

'Good lord ladies, bloody good job I'm here. Let's start by working out the wedding theme, shall we?'

'The theme? Do I need a theme?'

'It might be easier to understand what you want if we establish a theme.'

'Since when did you become a wedding planner?'

'I watched videos last night. They said you need a theme. They recommend doing a little test to help determine what sort of wedding you want. Say the first thing that comes into your head when I say these things....'

What feelings would you like the wedding to generate?

'Love and friendship, you know; lots of people having fun, flowers everywhere, lots to eat - obviously.'

'Great. That sounds lovely,' says Charlie.

'What is the budget?' asks Juan.

'I don't know. I need to talk to Ted.'

'OK, well, you must talk to Ted tonight. Promise me. We

can't really plan anything or book anything without knowing what sort of money we can spend.'

'I will.'

'In an ideal world, what venue would you have?'

'Oh lord, I don't know.'

'Ideal venue...off the top of your head.'

'Hampton Court Palace, with every one drifting out onto the riverside to drink cocktails in the evening sun.'

'Good lord, woman, you don't make it easy, do you? She wants a palace. A bloody palace!'

'You said ideal venue.'

'I know, chick, I'm only joking. Now, are there people coming who will need to stay overnight?'

'No'

'What would be your perfect wedding dress?'

'Simple, elegant, feminine. Mainly though, I'd just like one that fits.'

'You'll easily find one that fits; you've lost so much weight.'

'I know I've lost weight, but I'm still a size 14 and a big size 14. These wedding dress companies like their brides to be size 10 and 22 years old.'

'That's ridiculous. We're going to find you the perfect dress. You'll look more incredible than ever on your wedding day. Now - what would you like for the bridesmaids' dresses?'

'I'd like them to be flattering and fun.'

'Do you want a hen night?'

'God, yes.'

'Cake?'

'Yes'

'Flowers?'

'Yes - they will be taken care of my work.'

'Anything else we need to know?'

'No.'

'Good. Then we can do this. I will talk to Hampton Court Palace now and find out the process for having a wedding there, and I will find out the costs. It's just a small wedding party, so hopefully, they will have a spare room.'

'Do you really think I'll be able to get married there? I'd love that so much.'

'I have no idea, darling. I'm going to call them now.'

'Charlie, can you ring dress companies and book Mary some appointments this afternoon?'

'Mary, call Ted and talk to him about a budget, and see whether your mum is free for dress shopping today.'

Charlie and I stare at Juan as he issues his orders.

'Come on then. Go, go, go. Time is of the essence.'

And so we get stuck into our tasks, following the orders of the bossy Spaniard.

I manage to establish quite quickly that mum is free this afternoon.

'And she wants to come, does she?' asks Charlie.

'When I asked her that, she told me that nothing would stop her, and even if my father were on his deathbed, he'd have to cope for the afternoon without her while she came dress shopping.'

'That's a yes then. Good news. And - budget?' ***

'Ted said that we should make it a great day, so to book what I fancy but be a bit sensible. What does that mean?'

'Darling - it means we can go mad. Perfect. Now - Charlie, what have you found out?'

'Well, I don't have the best news. Mary is right, many of the dress shops only stock up to a size 14, and they told me that wedding dresses tend to come up a little smaller than average dresses because they are so heavily structured.'

'That's ridiculous. There must be some shops that cater to

normal-sized people. Have you made any appointments at all?'

'I tried to make some, but they told us to turn up. So I've got a list of shops here.'

'Good work,' says Juan, very formally. 'Now, my turn to share my news…it's good and bad. What would you like first?'

'Go on, get the bad news over with first,' I say.

'You can't book Hampton Court Palace. The place they do weddings is called the Great Hall, which is booked months and years in advance.'

'Oh. OK, but there's good news?'

'Yes, there is. There's a small gardening school in the palace grounds that could host a small wedding. It's only available until the end of August, but they will extend the booking period and let you book it on 1st September if you want.'

'Oh my God - that sounds great.'

'Yes, it is, but it's quite small, so you can't start inviting everyone you meet on a dog walk or down the pub.'

'Me? I'd never do that.'

Juan pulls out a picture of the small stone building on his phone. It's so perfect I want to cry. It's like it's in the Cotswolds or something…just grass and flowers everywhere, trees gently bowing towards the building, geese waddling nonchalantly across the path that leads towards it.

'And the river is just down here,' he says, pointing to the edge of the photograph. 'You could have your cocktails by the river in the evening.'

I launch myself at Juan and hug him until he struggles for breath. 'I love you,' I scream. 'I love you both so much.'

CHAPTER 5

We head off that afternoon - mum, Charlie, Juan, and I, packed into Charlie's little car, determined that we will return with a wedding dress to rival Kate Middleton's and four bridesmaids' dresses. I've decided to ask Charlie, Veronica, Karren, and Juan to be my bridesmaids. I know this is all wrong, I should have asked Ted's sister to be one, but I don't like her. I know that sounds brutal, but it's true. I've told Ted that we're keeping things small, but even if this were a wedding bigger than Prince William's, and I was having 450 bridesmaids, I still wouldn't want her standing next to me in a flouncy dress, criticising my every move.

The other thing is that I really want Juan to be a bridesmaid. I know what you're thinking - fine, have him as a bridesmaid, Mary, but you need to call him something different. You can't have a man being called a 'maid.'

Well, I thought of that, too. And I googled 'what is the male equivalent of a bridesmaid,' and you know what Google told me? It said that the male equivalent is a manservant.

Like Juan will ever be comfortable with me calling him my 'manservant.'

Apparently, 'maid' is short for 'maidservant,' so the male equivalent is 'manservant.'

I told Juan that we'd call him bridesman, but in all other ways, he'll be treated the same as the maids. He'll have a pink suit if we get the girls some pink dresses, and we'll be searching for a lavender suit if they are dressed in lavender. He says he doesn't mind what I put him in; he's thrilled to be there on my big day.

'You know that today might prove difficult, don't you?' says Charlie, easing the car into a parking space and pulling the hand brake on with such force that I think she will pull it off completely. 'You need a dress, three bridesmaids dresses, and a bridesman's suit, and you need to be able to pick them up in three weeks. I fear the time constraints might limit your options.'

'And add to that the fact that I'm not standard wedding dress size,' I say, wiggling my belly around to make the point.

'You're perfect bride size,' says mum. 'You were perfect before, but now you've lost weight; you look magnificent.'

Bless her. Mums are the best, aren't they?

Juan sits in the back of the car with me while mum is in the passenger seat. He leans over and kisses her lightly on the cheek.

'They better have dresses in our girl's size, or they'll have me to deal with,' he says. His aggressive tone reminds me of when I went into a clothes shop in Italy with him. The lady there was rude to me, saying they didn't have any clothes in my size. Of course, I was a lot bigger then, and many shops couldn't cater to me, so it wasn't a surprise, but Juan lost his mind. He did that *Incredible Hulk* thing of getting so angry I thought he would turn green and burst out of his clothes. He gave the woman a real telling-off.

'If they don't have any dresses in her size, we'll throw all their clothes on the floor and stamp all over them, won't we, Mrs. B?'

'We will,' she replies with a big smile. 'And we'll kick their windows in.'

'Mother,' I say. 'No need to encourage him.'

THE FIRST SHOP we go into is called 'Perfect Bride' in Kingston. I've noticed that most bridal shops give themselves naff names. I've no idea why they do this. Perhaps they're in some competition to see who can have the most vomit-inducing title. I point blank refused to contemplate a visit to *Pretty Little Bride* and *Angel on the Aisle* but was persuaded to give *Perfect Bride* a go by an increasingly fraught Charlie. 'You can't turn them all down just because of the names. They might have nice dresses.'

'Nope,' I said. 'We all know exactly what the dresses will be like with names like that.'

In the end, they forced me to pick one of them, and I went for *Perfect Bride*.

So, here we are…

'You're going to enjoy this shop. It's good fun,' says mum, as we all file in through the door. 'They ring a bell when you find a dress you like, and everyone applauds.'

'They do what?'

'They ring a bell. I think it's a lovely idea. It gets the whole shop involved.'

'Jesus Christ, mum. I don't want the whole damn shop involved.'

'I'm with Mary on this,' says Juan. 'It sounds like the very definition of hell. If the shop assistant starts ringing a bell, I will slap her.'

'I'd better not tell you that they sometimes do a guard of

honour as you leave the shop then. They hold flowers up for you to walk under and drop confetti down on top of you,' mum says. She drops this news on me when we're too far into the shop for me to turn round and run like the wind in the opposite direction.

'I will fight them all,' I say. 'Really - if we find a dress in there and they try that shit with me, I will fight them.'

'Mary Brown!' says mum. 'Stop being so coarse. And mind your language.'

In the end, we didn't need to worry about bells, guards of honour, or confetti, because the dresses were more hideous than I can ever convey to you in mere words. How on God's sweet earth do they get to call themselves *'Perfect Bride.'* It's in breach of the Trade Descriptions Act.

CHARLIE AND MUM try their best to encourage me throughout the shopping trip, with Charlie even resorting to lies and deception.

'It doesn't look *that* bad,' she says as I mince out of the changing room wearing a giant, crumpled-up net curtain that makes me look like Bjork in that swan dress she wore years ago. Only I'm a lot bigger than Bjork. My dress makes Bjork's look stylish and understated.

'You're right; it doesn't look *that* bad,' says mum, squinting slightly, presumably so she can't see me.

'Thanks, mum. That's what I always dreamed of people saying on my wedding day.' I say sarcastically. 'Here comes the bride, and she doesn't look *that* bad.'

'Come on, we're out of here,' says Juan. 'This is all too terrible; it's hurting my eyes.'

As we leave, we are offered sickly-sweet children's lollipops, which seem to sum up the whole experience neatly.

'There must be an elegant dress shop,' says Juan. 'A dress

shop in which there are clothes which don't make you look like a character from a pantomime.'

'Yes - there's *Cherished Brides*. We could walk there from here.'

'Come on then,' says Juan. 'Let's get our girl Cherished.'

To be fair, Cherished Brides is a lot better. They have dresses up to a size 30, making me feel great about my tiny size 14 body.

In addition to that, dresses can be rush ordered to arrive in three weeks. Wonderful. The only problem is that they have no samples in larger sizes. The sample sizes only go up to a size 12, which means that if I want one of the dresses, I will have to order it without knowing what it will look like when it arrives.

I try holding dresses up against me in the mirror, but it's tough to get a decent idea of what the dress will look like when it's on me.

Juan marches up to the sales assistant, his red boots clicking and clacking on the wooden floors like tap shoes. Minutes later, he comes click, clacking back. 'Come on, let's get out of here - this is hopeless.' he says. 'She advises that we go to *Engaged & Beautiful* in Guildford.'

'Yeah, that's on my list,' says Charlie. 'I called them, and they sound like they have a wide range of dresses, but they cater mainly for the older lady, and online the dresses look frumpy.'

'My God - they can't look worse than the creation that Perfect Brides put her in. Come on, let's go. Mrs. B, are you OK?'

'Oh, I'm fine,' says mum. 'I'm just astonished that none of the dresses fit. She's not big; she has a great figure. This is silly. I want her to have a lovely dress that she feels happy with for her special day. Surely there's somewhere better?'

'Let's head for Guildford, find a nice coffee shop, and

think things through,' says Charlie. 'Perhaps we just get a white or cream dress from a normal shop and jazz it up?'

'But I want a proper wedding dress,' I say. 'You know - like other brides have.'

'Yes, I know, lovely, and if that's what you want, that's what you'll have. I was just trying to think of an alternative. Just ignore me. Come on, let's go to Guildford.'

CHAPTER 6

Before I continue with the story of my valiant efforts to find a wedding dress, I have a question: have you ever been mistaken for someone else? More pertinently, has the person you're mistaken for been considerably older/bigger/odder-looking than you?

The reason I ask is that it just happened to me, and it was awful. A real shock.

I'm aware that I'm not a supermodel, not by a long way. But when we go for coffee in Guildford. I walk up to the counter and decide to get some lovely cakes too. It feels like the least I can do after all the hard work they have put into finding me the perfect dress. As I stand at the counter, an old lady approaches and says, 'Hello, how are you?'

'I'm fine,' I reply.

'Oh. I am sorry,' the lady says when she gets closer to me. 'I thought you were someone else. You look exactly like Glynis, who works in the cafe. Look - there she is now. You two could be twins.'

This is where it all goes wrong.

I look over at Glynis, waddling along behind the counter.

She is closer to 60 than 30, is entirely round (I'm guessing a size 24), and has white hair.

I'm 31, a size 14, and have blonde hair.

What the hell?

I don't share my horror story. Instead, I sulk. I sit in silence, with anger and bitterness growing within me as we sip our coffees and plan the next stage of what is becoming quite a mission. Who'd have thought that the battle to find a wedding dress that fits and doesn't make me look like one of those dolls that sits over toilet paper rolls would be so complicated?

After our coffee break, we go to *Engaged and Beautiful.* That is a terrible place, don't ever go there. *I'm Getting Married in the Morning!* smells of feet, and both *Love Me Do* and *Hitched* are full of scruffiness and joylessness. The more setbacks we have, and the more we come across shops with no dresses to fit me or delight me, the greater the sense of foreboding I have.

'If I don't manage to get a dress in this next shop, perhaps we should stop looking for today and find somewhere nice for lunch instead.'

'We will find something,' says Juan. 'No doubt about it. We're going to find a beautiful dress, and you're going to look stunning. Then we will have lunch.'

'But Charlie said earlier that I might have to wear a plain white dress if I don't find a wedding dress.'

'Ignore that. I say mad things sometimes; everyone says silly things from time to time,' Charlie says. 'Of course you will have a wedding dress, and it will be completely perfect.'

'OK,' I say.

'We just need to make sure that we find a shop with a little bell to ring,' says mum. 'I'll be disappointed if there's no ringing bell at the end of the day.'

'You know, if I can find a wedding dress I like after all this driving around, I don't care how many bloody bells they ring.'

The next shop is on the other side of Guildford. Walking through it on this warm mid-morning, I'm reminded of what a lovely place this is. I don't know whether you've been before, but it's beautiful - old world cobbled streets with lots of lively bars and restaurants and every clothes shop you could imagine.

I peer into the shop windows, as I always do, trying to imagine what I would buy from them if I were thin enough and rich enough to buy the clothes they sell.

The trouble is, I can't imagine the clothes on anything other than a slender body - that is what the shops are selling...clothes for a thin person. They couldn't be more overt about this. The mannequins are all size eight and wear expressions you never see in real life. They have this kind of intensified simper; sometimes a scowl and sometimes a vacant, far-away look as if contemplating the flowers on a poet's grave. They never look like average women going to work, the pub, or dropping the kids at school. Can anyone imagine themselves in these clothes when they look at the tortured faces of the mannequins?

'You're not going to find a wedding dress in there,' says mum, pulling me away from the window of surreal model faces. 'We must go down by the river to the wedding shop.'

I follow behind the others like the sulky pre-teen that I used to be...not quite dragging my feet but displaying juvenille resistance to the task. Even the bridge's beauty and the lovely park we walk through to get to the shop don't lift my mood.

But then we go round the bend, and suddenly, six rabbits tear off ahead of us, their little white tails furiously bobbing. I watch them as they speed along. Rabbits give good panic. You can hear them yelling, 'run for your lives, people are coming.' I find this curiously comforting. Little rabbits hopping along like we're in the middle of the countryside. For some reason, it feels like a lucky omen. I feel as if, despite all evidence to the contrary, a wedding dress will be found today.

'I'm going to find a dress in the next shop,' I say confidently.

'That's the spirit,' says mum.

We walk through the door, past the blank faces of the mannequins, and straight to the sales assistant.

'My name is Mary Brown,' I say. 'I'm size 14 and am getting married in a month. I realise that I'm supposed to order the dress four years before I meet the man I'm going to marry, but that's not the position I'm in. So I'd be very grateful if you could let me see every dress in size 14 that will be available in three weeks.'

'Of course,' says the lady. 'Please take a seat, and I'll bring you all the dresses I have. Champagne while you wait?'

'Yes,' we chorus.

Half an hour later, I've drunk two glasses of champagne, and I'm wearing the dress of my dreams. It's white, flattering, elegant, and gorgeous.

'I love it,' I say, with tears running down my face. 'I absolutely love it.'

We also find three bridesmaid dresses and a bridesmaid's suit in beautiful blue silk. Then we stand there, all of us looking into the mirror ahead while mum sobs in the corner.

'I think we've cracked it,' I say.

I had to buy a dress in size 16 in the end (damn!) and have it taken in a bit. The size 14 was too tight and the 16 quite loose, but the lady in the shop guaranteed the alternations could be done in time. I can't believe it: it's all coming together. I'm getting married!

. . .

It's lovely to be back home that evening. It was a successful day, but it was too hot to trudge around dress shops. My feet are burning, and even though I've had a shower, I still feel hot and sticky from all the walking around. So I'm on the sofa next to Ted, and we have brought the fan in from the bedroom to cool us down while we relax into the evening. The window is wide open behind us, but the air is still stultifying. It's like being in Greece or something, but if we were in Greece, there would be air conditioning and cool stone floors to keep the temperature under control.

'So, come on then…tell me about today - what happened, what did you buy, and what plans have you all been cooking up?' asks Ted.

'Well - as I said on the phone – the best news is that Juan found out that you can book the gardening school on the ground of Hampton Court Palace. It's this hidden gem: flowers everywhere, the river right next to it. I just love it. It's beautiful.'

'You've been to see it?'

'Not yet; I've seen pictures of it. I'm going to book to see it at the weekend. You'll come with me, won't you? Then if we love it as much as I think we will, we can make the booking.'

'OK, yes. Why don't you book it for first thing Saturday morning? I'm going to see Mike Williams for a few beers in the afternoon, but it would be great to see it first.'

'Oh God, Mike Williams? Why are you going to visit him? I hate him.'

'No, you don't. Mike's just a bit loud, that's all, but he's a nice guy.'

'Wasn't it him who was telling you to finish with me a couple of years ago?'

'He was, yes, but only because you were dating all these different men, and he thought you'd hurt me.'

'I wasn't 'dating all these different men'; I was doing

internet dating because you were dating horrible Dawn, and I was heartbroken.'

'I wasn't dating Dawn at all.'

'She told me you two were dating.'

'I know she did, but she was lying. It was a horrible time for us both, and I understand why you went internet dating, but you must understand that my friends were worried.'

'I can't imagine Mike being worried about anything other than where his next pint's coming from.'

'He's a good guy. You haven't spent a lot of time with him. He likes you, really.'

'Yeah, right.'

'I'd like the two of you to get on because I was thinking of asking him to be my best man.'

'What? No, please, no. Mike? Why Mike?'

'I've known him since school. He's one of my oldest friends.'

'Oh, God. But won't he just get hammered and try to chat up all the bridesmaids?'

'Yes, I imagine he will. Isn't that what a best man is supposed to do?'

'No, he's supposed to support and look after you and want the best for you. That guy's only interested in himself.'

'He's not. He has a big, important job; he knows how to get things done.'

'He's in the police.'

'Yes, and he's high up in the Met. He's a Detective Chief Inspector. He does lots of sneaky-beaky undercover stuff. He's very well-respected.'

'I didn't realise he was that senior. What is the Met thinking of? I wouldn't trust him as far as I could throw him. Anyway, it doesn't matter what job he does. He doesn't want you to get married because he wants you to be young, free, and single so you can go off drinking together and pick up women.'

'He doesn't. He likes you. Stop worrying about everything.'

'Has he said that he likes me?'

'Not in so many words, but everyone likes you, Mary.'

'And you think he's such a great person to be your best man?'

'Yes, I do.'

Mike was one of Ted's great rugby buddies, and they spent a lot of time together before Ted was injured and had to give up the sport. They got drunk and got laid in every town they played. I know they were close mates back then, but I also know that Mike was disappointed when Ted and I got together because he no longer had a drinking partner on tap. I never liked the dismissive way Mike treated me, as if I wasn't good enough for his beloved friend and as if I was stopping their fun.

'So, come on then - tell me what else you did today. You know how much I adore to hear about your dress shopping.'

'It was good,' I say, trying not to think about Mike and his horrible sneery, pompous face.

'Just good?'

'No, it was great. I got a dress I like, and I'm delighted with it.'

'Oh good. So, do you have it now? Is it hiding somewhere?'

'No, I had to order it, then it needs adjustments. Remarkably, it needs to be taken ***in***. Imagine that! I hope you like me in it.'

You'll look gorgeous, whatever you wear. I can't wait to marry you, Mary Brown.'

'Oh, Ted, I can't wait to marry you either. I love you so much.'

He kisses me at that point. It's a lovely, slow, tender kiss, but I'm too irritated to enjoy the moment properly. Bloody Mike will be at my big day. I don't like that guy one bit.

'You know, you should go and sort your suit out soon,' I say to Ted. 'You may find that suits must be booked and organised in advance. You should check.'

'Really? What bloke is going to buy a suit a month early?'

'Wedding blokes. Everything seems to have to be done months and months in advance.'

'OK, I'll talk to Mike about it on Saturday, and we'll make a plan.'

CHAPTER 7

'We've sorted it,' say, Juan and Charlie, giggling like naughty toddlers as they stand before me, clutching onto one another. 'We're going on a long hen weekend to Crete next weekend. You can't say no.'

'We haven't got time for a long weekend. I've got a wedding to organise.'

'Yes - there's time. Flowers are sorted, the dress is sorted, the venue is sorted.'

'But no catering, invitations, wedding gifts list, or other stuff. And I can't possibly go next weekend, that'll mean coming back a couple of days before my wedding. I'm getting married on Tuesday.'

'So? We'll ensure everything's done before we go, and your mum will take over Wedding Day HQ while we're away. We've spoken to her, and she's keen to help.'

'Are you sure?'

'Yes. She thinks it's great that we're taking you away. You've just got to tell us who you'd like us to invite to the hen weekend, and we'll get it all sorted.'

'Blimey. Are you sure we shouldn't just have a hen night in this country? Or a day out, or something?'

'No. We love you, and we're taking you away - it's only for a couple of days, and there's still time before we go. So it'll be fine, love, honestly.'

'OK. I guess it would be great fun.'

'It will be amazing fun, and you'll come back with a lovely tan for your wedding day.'

'I don't have to invite Ted's sister, do I?'

'No, we're putting a ban on inviting anyone because you think you ought to. This is going to be great fun. Only the best people get to come.'

'OK then - well... me, you two, Veronica from Fat Club, Karren from work, and perhaps I'll invite Maria, who I walk Elvis with. I mean, she's quiet, but I think she'd love to be invited, and I really like her.'

'Sounds good to me,' says Juan. 'If you really like her, she should come.

THAT EVENING, I run the hen weekend idea past Ted.

'I'm concerned that it's all a bit close to the wedding,' I say.

'That's good,' he replies. 'You'll have everything done, and you'll be able to go away and relax before the big day.'

'But what if there are last-minute hitches?'

'You said your mum would keep an eye on things. I will, too.'

'Are you really sure you think I should do this?'

'Sweetheart, absolutely, 100% I think you should do this. Now tell me – who will be going?'

'I'd like my bridesmaids to be there, but I'd also like Maria to come. She's lovely, sweet, and kind. She's good company but very shy.'

'Will it be odd that she'll be the only one going who's not a bridesmaid?'

'No, I don't think so. I haven't known Maria that long, so she wouldn't expect to be a bridesmaid, but I think she'd appreciate the chance to come with us for a long weekend.'

'OK, who else?'

'Are you saying that you don't remember who my bridesmaids are?'

'All I can remember is that Charlie and Juan are bridesmaids.'

'Juan is a bridesman.'

'Of course.'

'Karren Spencer from work is one bridesmaid. You remember her, don't you? She's very sophisticated and professional by day and a wild, drunken lunatic by night.'

'Oh yes. Yes, I remember.'

Karren is like a head girl. She is a master at organising everything in the store. She's very punctual, practical, and punctilious about detail. Which is great... I'm all in favour of that. Having someone there who checks and double-checks everything and keeps me out of trouble suits me down to the ground. Details are not something I'm great at, to be fair.

The thing with Karren that I love, and why she has a special place in my heart, is that she changes entirely after a few drinks. She becomes raucous, knocks back beer like a sailor, and leads the singing and dancing. Honestly, she's like Jekyll and Hyde. I remember her standing on a table, belting out 'Like a Virgin' at the top of her lungs once (with lots of booty shaking and boob thrusting), and I thought we were going to get chucked out of the bar. In the end, it took two bouncers to get her down. She's bloody wild. Then she wakes up, and she's back to being Corporate Karren again with her clipboard and obsession with everything being in order.

'She sounds like trouble. You should invite her.

'She's a loony. Perfect for a hen weekend.'

'Who else?'

'I'm going to invite beautiful Veronica.'

'Veronica from Fat Club?'

'Yep, the very same. She goes by the grand name of Veronica Bronks-Whalley these days, and she lives in the heart of Paris in a sun-dappled apartment overlooking the Seine. She married a rich and generous man. I should be doing that instead of messing around with you.'

'Oy, cheeky. You can keep well away from rich Frenchmen and stay right here with me.'

'Oh, OK then. It'll be nice to catch up with Veronica. I haven't seen much of her since she upped and left for Paris, but we always WhatsApp. She's lost a load of weight now and looks amazing.'

'You've lost a load of weight and look amazing.'

'Yeah, but she looks properly amazing.'

'So do you.'

'Stop being nice to me, or I will beat you up.'

'Come on, then,' he says. And that's where discussions of the hen weekend temporarily stop. We play fight, then play kiss, then really kiss. Then we go to bed.

Hours later, we're lying in each other's arms, enjoying the cool breeze from the fan. Elvis is sitting on the end of the bed, and all is well with the world.

'Did we go through all the people going on the hen week-end?' asks Ted.

'Yes. Charlie and Juan are the other two, and you don't need me to tell you anything about those two nutters.'

'And look – right on queue. It's Juan calling me.'

'Hello stranger,' I say.

'We need to discuss the dress code for the weekend,' he says sharply.

'There's a dress code?'

'Yes. In fact, there's a theme for the whole weekend.'

'Go on...'

'The Sound of Music.'

'Oh, that sounds fun,' I say. I was slightly afraid when Juan mentioned a dress code. I thought we'd all be dressed as carrots all weekend or in clothes from the 1970s. But a Sound of Music theme? Oh, I like that a lot.

'And can we play Drink-Along-A-Sound-of-Music?'

'Of course we can. We'll each be a different character, and you have a drink every time your character appears on the screen. If your character talks to another character, you change drinks with that person. Any time any player goes upstairs or sings, everyone drinks.'

'Amazing. So amazing.'

'We've talked to everyone on the invitation list, and they're all coming. There's definitely no one else you want to invite, is there? What about when you went to Wales to that funeral and met all those people you became friends with?'

'No, I won't invite them. I want the hen weekend to be small.'

'OK, well, that's sorted then. We're going to Crete. The theme is 'The Sound of Music,' and we will have the best time imaginable.'

So, my hen weekend is all sorted, flowers are being sorted by work, the dress and bridesmaids' outfits are ordered, now Ted and I need to visit the wedding venue, and we can get that booked and tick it off the list.

'Do you know where it is?' says Ted as we walk through the palace's main gates.

'All she said was to walk round the maze to the back of the palace, and you'll see it signposted.'

'Well, the signs say the maze is up here, so I guess that's where we should head.'

It's quite a long walk, to be fair, and we approach it all wrong so that we walk all the way around the palace, but when we find it, it's well worth the trek.

It is the most beautiful place, tucked away in the trees, near the river, and surrounded by flowers. Inside the building, it's pretty basic, but all the more lovely because of that. I can picture how incredible it will look when it is decorated with freshly-cut flowers and all the tables set for the wedding breakfast.

'White and creams everywhere,' I say, suddenly turning into Laurence Llewellyn-Bowen. 'Organza, silk and voile.'

'Do you want it?' says Ted, ignoring my haberdashery-related cries.

'Oh yes,' I say. 'Imagine the linen tablecloths, fabulous candles, and white lilies everywhere.'

We decide to book it on the spot, and I feel so happy about everything.

'You're the best,' I say to Ted. 'I mean it. You're the absolute best person I've ever met. And I am so glad that we're getting married.'

'Me too,' he says, somewhat shocked at the sudden outburst of emotion. But I can't help it. Every time we organise something to do with the wedding, it's as if another plank has been put in place as we build towards the big day. And the big day is all about Ted and me being together forever and ever. And though I'm delighted with the day we're building, the truth is that it doesn't really matter. If the flowers aren't the right shade of pink, or the tablecloths aren't high-grade linen, it simply doesn't matter. Not at all.

. . .

AWAY FROM THE WEDDING PLANNING, I start packing straight away for the hen weekend, leaving my bag open on the side and throwing things into it every day, so I don't have any last-minute packing to contend with.

Ted noses around the bag, surveying the contents like he's a customs officer on drug control.

'What are these?' he asks, teasing a pair of lacy knickers out of the case. 'What do you need these for?'

'Oh, for goodness sake, I like them; no one else will see them.'

'No, they won't because I'm taking them out.'

Ted takes the lacy number out and replaces it with pair of enormous royal blue pants.

'Where the hell did you find those? I think they're my old PE knickers.'

'In that draw.'

He points to the drawer where I keep my socks and old things that I never wear anymore but have - for some reason - decided to keep.

'You're jealous, aren't you? You don't want me going off to the sunshine with the girls in case I meet some gorgeous, tanned young man in Crete.'

'No, I'm not at all jealous, and I want you to have a lovely time, but I want you to have a lovely time while wearing proper sturdy underwear. I know what these Greek men are like.'

'Put whatever you like in the case, love. I probably won't wear any underwear once I'm out there.'

'Oy!' he says, grabbing me and pulling me into him. 'You make sure you are wearing the sturdiest underwear at all times.'

'OK,' I say. 'Big, blue pants it is.'

He kisses me lightly on the lips. 'I mean it when I say I hope you have a good time. Make sure you relax, forget about all the planning and organising, and enjoy your friends' company.'

'I will,' I say. 'Everyone has been so kind and helpful that there's little to be done. I'm so excited.'

'Me too,' he says, lifting me into his arms. 'I love you so much. I can't wait for you to be my wife.'

He puts me down on the floor, and I remove the blue PE pants from my bag, throwing the lacy ones back in. Ted leans over and throws them back out again.

Honestly, he can be such an idiot at times. It's not as if I'm likely to go off with someone else while I'm on my hen weekend.

'What are you doing for your stag night?' I ask.

'We're just going to the pub.'

'Really? I'd have thought Mike would have fixed up a wild weekend in Amsterdam for you.'

'Yeah, he's not the best organiser in the world. The pub will be great; we'll just get drunk, tell daft stories, and get a curry. I'm delighted with that.

All I want is for you to have the best time with your friends and enjoy the sunshine and the cocktails, but what do you have to remember at all times?'

'Wear the big, blue pants.'

'Good girl.'

CHAPTER 8

I don't know what you're doing today, but I'm dressed as a nun walking through Heathrow Airport while people all around me stare as if I have two heads. Quite how I get myself into these ludicrous predicaments is beyond me. However, it's not even my fault this time, and it's not of my choosing... I've been forced into the outfit as part of the Sound of Music theme that will colour my hen weekend celebrations.

Right now, though, I feel like a fool. People look at me and sometimes offer small bows, and I can't help but respond by nodding gently or putting my hands into a prayer position.

'They think you're a real nun,' says Charlie.

'Yeah, do you think it's the lipstick, the handbag, or the pink shoes persuading them?'

'All three,' she says, putting her hands into a prayer position and nodding gently.

'So why aren't we all dressed as nuns? There are lots of nuns in The *Sound of Music*, not just one,' I say to Juan and Charlie.

'Yes, but there's only one nun at the start – Julie Andrews. That's you. You may feel all alone now, but we'll all be wearing nuns' habits when we get out there and plan our big night out,' he says, causing the passengers next to us to swing around to take a closer look.

'Bless you, my child,' says Juan, bowing his head.

His efforts to impersonate a nun would have more impact if he weren't male, weren't wearing a sleeveless t-shirt with 'I like boys' on it, and if he weren't wearing glittery purple eyeshadow.

'When are Maria and Karren coming?' asks Charlie. 'I'd have thought Karren would be here first, clutching itineraries for the weekend and waving her clipboard in the air. The only thing I can remember about that woman is that she is like a head girl - organised and efficient.'

'I told them to go through check-in and that we'd catch up with them on the other side. Veronica is travelling from Paris, and she'll meet us at the airport in Crete.'

'You're so organised, Juan. I'm seeing a whole, new side to you.'

'Yeah, well – don't get used to it. I'm never organising anything again.'

I lift the skirts of my habit to walk forward and join Charlie and Juan in the queue.

'I love the way you do that,' says Charlie. 'That habit quite suits you.'

'I must be honest, I'm quite enjoying wearing it. I don't have to bother with doing my hair because the wimple covers it, and all this material covers my big tummy and bottom. I might never take it off.'

'You might have to take it off when you go through customs,' says Charlie. 'It's so big and baggy that you could be storing anything inside it. I bet you'll get taken to one side for questioning.'

'They might give me a strip search.'

'Lucky girl,' says Juan. 'I might put one on.'

'No, seriously, I think I should take it off. You're right, Charlie; I could have a dozen guns stuck up here. They're bound to want to frisk me.'

'You're not taking it off. The rule of the hen weekend is that you must always be dressed as a nun.'

'I thought the rule of the hen weekend was *what goes on a hen weekend, stays on a hen weekend.*'

'Yes, that as well. You'll be fine to wear it through customs; just tell them you're a nun, and they'll leave you alone,' says Juan.

'I promise I will always wear it once we get to Crete but do I want to tangle with these security officers?'

'Yes, some of them are gorgeous. Be a nun,' says Juan, and for some reason, I say 'OK,' and head through the scanning machine and to the queue for passport control with my wimple firmly in place.

'Well done, lovely. Just the passport checker to get passed now, and you'll have done all the security checks while nunned up.'

I step forward and smile beatifically at the security officer.

'Hen weekend?' he asks.

'Yes, sorry. My friends insist that I wear this.'

'Have a good time,' he says, handing back my passport.

'What did he say?' asks Juan, catching up with me as we walk through to departures. 'I heard him talking to you.'

'He told me that I must not impersonate a nun. So I told him to piss off.'

'Wow. Did you really? Is that what you said? Charlie - come here...Mary told the security guard to piss off.'

'Of course I didn't, you lunatic. Security man asked me if I was going on a hen weekend, and I said I was.'

'Oh my God, I thought you'd sworn at the man. Come on. Let's go and find Karren and Maria. It's drink time.'

'At 10am?'

'It's your hen weekend. Drinking is always allowed. This is positively late to start drinking on a hen weekend. Now, Charlie - text the other two, tell them to meet us in the bar, and let's get on it quickly before the flight takes off.'

CHAPTER 9

We land at Heraklion airport in Crete and feel that surge of heat as we exit the plane. Walking down those steps onto the tarmac is no mean feat in a billowing habit, but the unique feeling of foreign warmth makes it all worthwhile. It's a beautiful sort of heat, isn't it? One full of promise and laden with the prospect of excitement and joy. Not like when it gets hot in England and the trains stop, your feet swell, and everyone starts slowly melting.

When we walk outside the terminal building, we find ourselves in that heat that you can almost see...do you know the one I mean? Like the air is shaking from the torridness of the temperature, creating a shimmering haze. Or perhaps it's the alcohol? I must admit that I'm feeling a little drunk; not entirely out of my mind but starting to sway. I had a couple of drinks at the airport, then another couple on the plane. I'm not used to all this daytime drinking.

'Welcome in Crete. I taxi man. Hello all,' says a man in a white shirt and camel-coloured jacket, having leaped from his cab in a remarkably spritely manner for a man who must be approaching 70. 'I take bag from the ladies now.'

He reaches down to take our bags.

'Actually, I'm a man,' says Juan.

Out taxi driver steps back and looks again, thrown by the deep voice.' But you have sparkle eye, like a lady.'

'Yes, well, I'm a sparkled-eyed man.'

I imagine that Juan spends much of his time correcting those who misgender him.

Then the cab driver turns to me: 'My holy sister. I am not worthy,' he says. He bends before me, holding the cross around his neck, nestled in his dark chest hair. He looks at me with such reverence and love that I don't know what to do.

'Thank you,' I say, lightly touching his shoulder as if transferring some sort of strength and power to him. I feel like such a fraud. I forgot how religious some countries can be. I don't want anyone to feel like I'm mocking them.

The bags are in the boot, we're all in the car, and Juan has pulled out the bottle of rhubarb gin that he bought at the airport and is transferring it into the small plastic cups that Karren brought with her.

'Down in one,' he shouts as we knock back the drink.

The driver looks astonished.

I don't know what to say. I toy with the idea of saying *the blood of Christ* to make him think that this is a religious exercise of some kind, but that seems even more disrespectful, so I smile warmly at him, and when my cup is refilled, I knock that back as well.

I feel so relaxed in my seat, with the sun on my skin, but the air conditioning keeps me cool. I lean back a little as the sun hits a particularly lovely spot right on the side of my neck. The cab edges forward, and now the sun hits the small of my back. It has a soothing, soporific effect. I feel like lying down and sleeping as the sun warms me, one bit at a time.

'That's called apricity,' says Juan.

'What is? The airport?'

'No, that there - what you're doing...feeling the warmth of the sun on you when the rest of you is cold.'

'Oh wow, they have a word for that in Crete?'

'No - that's the English word, you lemon.'

'Really? I've never heard it before.'

'It's a good word, isn't it? It's usually used to describe the sun in winter, but I'm sure it applies just as well to an air-conditioned car. I had this boyfriend once; he was married to an English teacher and would teach me a new word every day because she taught him a new word every day. I'm not sure she would have taught him so many lovely words if she knew he was using them to woo a man.'

'I think you should teach us a word a day, Juan. By the time we return, we'll have a plethora of words to throw around like confetti,' says Veronica, managing to be kind to Juan while immaculately displaying her superior vocabulary.

'It sounds like you have enough words of your own,' says Maria.

We continue the journey to our hotel along wide, main roads, then soon we are in the countryside. Charlie pulls a pair of binoculars from her bag and watches out of the open window as we sweep along next to lush, green fields while the driver talks to us in his superb, broken English.

'Is good time of year,' he says. 'Look at it. Lovely time. Cheers and smiles for the olives.'

'Yay!' we all reply, raising our little glasses.

'Charlie, what on earth did you bring binoculars for? Are you planning to do some bird watching while we're here?'

'No. Just thought a pair of bins might be useful.'

'You're going to perve at all the Greek men by the pool, aren't you?'

'Oh yes,' she says, laying them down for a second. 'You'll all want to borrow them when there are half-naked Greek men to ogle.'

The driver can sense the cheery mood in the cab, so he leans over to fiddle with the dial and provides us with a little party.

'Here is a song of you country,' he says, as Madonna's 'Like a Virgin' bursts out. We all scream as if we're at a rock concert and sing along in our loudest voices. The gin is being passed, we're dancing in our seats, and life is good.

I peek a sideways look at our driver. He smiles and glances into the mirror, checking out Veronica. He is in his late 60s, at a guess. Wide-shoulders, fleshy, and with magnificent eyes the colour of amber. Seriously, his eyes are incredible, as if he were wearing contact lenses made of glistening stones.

We reach the town centre, where a petite lady in a lovely red dress stands in front of a group, pointing out various local attractions. She's clearly a tour guide.

The driver pulls up beside her, rolls down all the windows, and turns the music up full blast so that none of the tourists can hear her. The song has changed, and Livin' On A Prayer is now screeching across the pretty town square.

The lady turns round, fury etched across her face, she barks at him, but he just starts beeping the horn to add to the cacophony of noise.

She turns to stare at him again, but this time begins walking towards the car, shouting at him in Greek.

'Uh oh,' he says, driving off at top speed while laughing heartily. 'This woman, she is a police officer. She do tours of the area at weekend. Now she is furious.'

'Oh lord. Are you going to get in trouble?'

'Ah, no. Me too pretty for getting in trouble.'

'Our driver is insane,' says Karren.

'Bonkers,' says Veronica.

'Bonkers for love with you,' says the driver.

Then we all drink a little bit more gin.

By the time we get to the hotel, I'm drunk. OK, maybe that's a bit of an exaggeration, but I'm undoubtedly tipsy. I'm smiling, laughing, and generally confused about where I am and who I am. I know I gave my number to the taxi driver and told him to come out with us for the evening. So yeah - I'm pretty drunk. I need water and to rest on a comfortable bed in an air-conditioned room for a while.

Happily, the hotel we're in is AMAZING. Even in my smiley, drunken state, I can see how great Hotel Xenia is, and I tell Agata, the owner, with great flourishes of my hands, and by nearly falling over her, that this is the best hotel in the whole world ever. 'Wow,' I say, as she points out the most mundane details.

'This is the door through to the bedrooms.'

'Oh wow. A door. Amazing. Bedrooms. Yeah. Wow,' I hear myself saying.

When she shows me to my room, which is the grandest room in the hotel, I almost weep with joy. I'm embarrassed to recount this all to you, but I get very emotional and hug he, thanking her for everything she's doing for me in my life.

She backs off quite a bit, so I throw myself into the air and land on the bed with an almighty cracking sound. I think I've broken it. And from the look on the woman's face, she thinks I have, too.

Agata has given me the best room because I am the bride-to-be. The others are cramped in, three in a room, to be able to afford to house me in luxury. I'm very touched, so I naturally hug them all, tell them how much I love them, and wish I was marrying them instead of Ted.

The rest of the rooms are next to mine, and our balconies sit beside one another. Agata has backed off, so she is out of reach and doesn't have to endure any more of my emotional hugs. From her safe distance, she explains that the barriers between the balconies can be lifted to create one extended patio. It should be big enough for us to put a table out and eat there, lie in the sun or have drinks in the evening. This news prompts further outcries of delight from me before I collapse back onto the bed and fall asleep.

It's 6pm when I wake up to see Charlie, Juan, Karren, Veronica, and Maria looking down at me. It takes me a second before I realise I'm on my honeymoon. They are all dressed for a night out, and I'm in my knickers and my wimple. Somewhere along the way, I appear to have thrown off my habit.

'Party time, sleeping beauty,' says Veronica.

'Yesh,' I say, sitting up and rubbing my hands over my face in a very unattractive way. I can't imagine how awful I must look.

'I just need to have a bath, then I'll come out,' I say.

'I'll run it,' says Juan, skipping into the bathroom. 'Wow! This bathroom is gorgeous. Just look at all these lotions and potions,' he says. Seconds later, a lovely floral aroma snakes through from the bathroom.

'It's going to be very bubbly and smelly,' he says

'Just how I like it.'

I clamber off the bed and walk into the bathroom, promising everyone I won't be long.

'Don't be!' says Karren. 'We've got a strict timetable to

follow, and remember to take your wimple off before you get into the water.'

I glance at her, and she smiles. 'Not really. No strict schedules on honeymoon.'

Thank God for that. I'm not really in a bossy Karren from work sort of mood.

When I kick out the hens and get to the bathroom, the bath is brimming with gorgeous bubbles and scents.

I begin to lower myself into it but realise that the tub has completely overfilled and that if I recline, the water will flow over the side. I'm unsure what course of action to take. This happens quite often to me, probably because I underestimate my displacement. In my head, I have the figure of a damsel fly rather than that of a hefty overeater.

At this point, there are two options... the first, and by far the most sensible is to swiftly exit the bath, unplug, and wait till the water recedes to a safe level. But I don't do that. Oh no. Instead, I take the plug out and then gradually lower myself, calculating the rate of recline so that the water level stays constant. This requires quite a lot of skill and fine muscle control. Unfortunately, the bath drains very slowly, so I have to balance and use the muscles in my arms to slowly lower myself. Nevertheless, there's a tremendous sense of achievement when I sit in the bath with no water sploshed over the edge.

Anyway, I thought I'd share that with you. It's just another of those ways in which you can transform the ordinary into the beautiful. Nothing great was ever achieved without some risk-taking.

'ARE you ever coming out of there,' comes a voice from the balcony, just as I'm relaxing. What shocking timing. I've finally finished my life meets art experiment, and I'm being called to party.

I look up to see Charlie at the door.

'Get out of the bath and come and play,' she shouts

Then other faces appear at the door.

'Come on, you've been ages,' they say.

I want to explain the slow lowering into the water and how time-consuming experiments can be, but I fear I may be mocked.

'For God's sake! I'm naked here,' I shout. 'Go and amuse yourselves on the balcony. I'll be there soon.'

'We're not looking,' they say. 'We want you to come out and play. We want to have food and drink and have a fab time.'

'Give me 10 minutes,' I reply, but that does nothing to calm them down.

'You've got soooo boring since you got engaged,' they say. 'Get out of the bath and come and play.'

'OK, OK,' I say, laughing to myself as I ease myself out of the lovely warm, bubbly tub and attempt to wrap a tiny towel around myself. Why do hotel managers buy towels that are so tiny? Who could possibly dry themselves effectively with this scrap of material?

'I'll meet you on the balcony in five minutes; I just need to get dressed.'

I put on a pair of black capri pants, a white t-shirt, and some gorgeous mock-Chanel ballet pumps. I think I look sophisticated and a little bit French as I throw a black jacket over my shoulders and saunter onto the balcony.

'What are you wearing?' shrieks Juan. 'I mean - in the name of all that is holy, what are you wearing?'

'I'm trying to look sophisticated and ever-so-slightly Parisienne,' I reply.

'Yeah, you're not in Paris now; you're on your hen weekend. So off you go, Sister Mary.'

'I have to wear that nun's habit all the time??'

'ALL THE TIME,' they chorus.

So much for looking stylish. My one and only attempt to look like an 'it' girl from Paris, and they've sent me back inside to change.

While slipping into my habit and adjusting my wimple over my sparkly earrings (that's a sentence you'll only ever hear on a hen weekend), I hear the clank of bottles on the balcony. They have obviously been out and bought loads of booze. I doubt I will be sober very often on this trip.

'Hooray!' they shout when I appear on the balcony dressed appropriately.

'Lovely to see you, sister. May peace be with you.'

'Thank you, dear people,' I reply as they hand me a shot. I've only just sobered up from a morning of drinking, and now I'm about to throw back a shot. I drink it, of course, because to refuse would be churlish and not in keeping with the great traditions of hen weekends.

'We have found a wonderful cafe. It's gorgeous,' says Charlie, offering to refill my shot glass. 'The couple who run it are so friendly. We've arranged to go back down there later to buy food and more drink. We thought we'd party on the balcony tonight, then hit the town tomorrow evening. The food they've got in that place is out of this world. Do you want to come down with me?'

'Sure,' I say.

'Ready to go now? Everyone here is starving.'

'I'm all dressed up and raring to go,' I say. 'I'll just slip on my pink mules.'

'Spoken like a true nun,' says Charlie, grabbing her handbag and following me into my room.

CHAPTER 10

We walk out of Xenia hotel and into gentle sunshine. It's not boiling hot now, but it is still warm, which invigorates me, as warm evenings often do. I attempt to roll up the sleeves of the habit, so I can feel the sun on my arms, but these outfits aren't designed for sunbathing, and the material doesn't want to stay up.

'Do you think you can get summer habits? Perhaps with short sleeves or even halter necks?' I ask Charlie.

'Er, no,' she replies.

The cafe is at the bottom of a flight of rickety concrete steps, with colourful, aroma-filled plants and flowers on either side that intrude onto the steps so that you walk through them as you tiptoe down. It makes the descent very charming but not easy. I don't suppose they get too many nuns in here; the steps certainly aren't designed with floor-brushing habits, nor do they accommodate the high-heeled mules I have chosen to wear. Next time I come down, it will be in flip-flops or trainers. At the bottom of the steps, we proceed onto a beautiful veranda overlooking the sea.

'This is CeeCees,' says Charlie.

'Wow.'

The area is filled with pots and plants. There are loads of tables with umbrellas in every colour under the sun. On the seats, there are colourful cushions. The whole place is a vision of rainbow loveliness, with the sea lapping up against the wall next to it.

'I love this,' I say. 'How did you find it? It's beautiful.'

'Maria's mum recommended it,' says Charlie. 'Isn't it wonderful?'

Music is playing, gentle chatter emerges from inside the cafe, and a gorgeous barbecue smell snakes its way through the air. It is so delicious that I can feel my mouth watering.

'Hello, you are back,' says a man in a white apron. He couldn't be anything but Greek with his handsome, swarthy, dark looks, hairy arms, and super glossy hair. 'And you have brought a beautiful friend with you. A lady of the cloth. I and enchanted.'

'Hello, I'm Mary,' I say.

He crosses himself and tells me that he is pleased that a friend of the Lord is visiting him. I'm not sure what to say to this; it seems almost cruel to tell him that I've dressed up for fun and not because I have any religious conviction, so I just smile at him, nod gently, and behave as I think one should in the circumstances.

'We need to buy a lot of food,' says Charlie. 'I have a balcony full of starving people out there.'

'You are in the right place,' says the man. 'I am Cosmos. This my cafe. I work here with my beautiful lady wife, Calista. Two people with names beginning with 'C,' so the café is CeeCee's. You understand?'

'Yes, of course,' I say. 'It's lovely to meet you. You speak English so beautifully.'

'Ah, yes. English essential. Must to speak English if to run a cafe. Look now - here come my wife.'

A lady walks out from the kitchen, wiping her hands on her apron. She has a great mane of hair - thick, blond, and curly, tumbling over his shoulders. Her face is tanned, her jeans are tight, and her figure is fantastic. These two are the most beautiful couple.

We all shake hands, and I am treated to a slight bow and a declaration of love for the church and God. But, once again, I feel a complete fraud for accepting the sentiments without explaining that I'm in fancy dress. I'm not going to be very good at handling all this. I didn't realise it was such a religious country and that people would be delighted to see me. Perhaps I should get a sign letting everyone know that I'm dressed up for my hen weekend; I'm not a nun, so there's no need to treat me with such reverence.

'Come, come. You can choose which foods, then we make it while you have a drink.' Cosmos leads us into the café and to a counter with the most delicious foods beneath it. A sign informs us that this is the takeaway area; a lively bar and another smaller restaurant are next to it. But there's no doubt that the main action is outside, where dozens of people sit, watching the sea on the beautiful terrace while they eat.

'So, what can I get for you?'

'I want it all,' I say. 'I can't choose. It's all too delicious.'

Cosmos laughs, throwing his head back, revealing a small tattoo on the left-hand side of his neck. It's barely visible beneath a layer of stubble. When he sees me looking, he hastily covers it with his hand.

'Would you like me to put together a package of some of our finest foods,' he says. 'You let me know what you like and don't like, and I will choose a feast.'

'A feast is exactly what we want,' says Charlie, rubbing her hands together. 'How many people?'

'Six,' I say. 'Six starving people, so maybe cater for seven.'

'I shall provide a feast for six lovely ladies, with some extras thrown in as a gift from CeeCee's.'

'Perfect,' I say. 'Though it's not six ladies. It is five ladies and one man.'

'Oh, what a lucky man. He is a priest?'

'No, no. Juan's not a priest. Not a priest at all. He couldn't be less like a priest.'

Charlie titters beside me at the thought of anyone confusing Juan with a priest.

'Will you need any wine to go with your food?'

'Do we need more wine?' I ask Charlie. 'I'm not sure how many bottles they bought earlier.'

What do you think? asked Charlie. 'Yes, six bottles of the wine we bought earlier,' she says, causing me to gasp a little.

'I thought tonight was the relaxed evening in.'

'Yeah, a relaxed but very drunken evening in. We need a drink. For heaven's sake, you're dressed like a nun, and everyone is bowing to you. You'll need a couple of glasses to get you through.'

'You are dressed like a nun?' says Cosmos. 'So not real nun?'

'No, I'm not really a nun. Sorry, I didn't mean to fool you or anything.'

'It doesn't matter,' he says, shouting over to Calista in Greek, presumably telling her it's OK to swear.'

Then he turns back to me.

'You must be careful,' he says. 'If you are in a nun's costume, religious people will be very cross. They maybe come running after you.'

I laughed at this comment. Not out loud so he could hear me, but I did think the idea that religious fanatics might come running after me in the street waving sticks was amusing.

'Now, you two sit down and have some snacks before you return while I prepare the feast for you.'

'Oh yes, that would be excellent,' I say. 'I'm starving.'

'No problem.'

While preparing our feast, he puts a spread on the table in front of us that would be enough food for the whole hen party. Right before me is a large pizza with delicious ham and truffle oil. I take a delicate sliver of it and think I might explode with delight. It's delicious. The ham is gorgeous and spicy, and the oil is terrific…thick and sweet, not like eating an oily pizza at home, but somehow light and tasty.

But I know it's a bad idea for me to put on any weight while I'm here because there's no time to get my wedding dress adjusted when I get back, so I reach over with my napkin to blot out some of the excess grease from the top of it. Charlie watches me.

'If I look skinny tomorrow, don't be alarmed,' I tell her. 'I have just blotted away about one-tenth of the oil off my pizza; I might fade away to nothing.

'I'll keep an eye on you,' she promises.

'Here you go,' says Cosmos, handing us a large basket brimming with food. 'You take that. I will come with the wine.'

'It's so kind of you to help us,' I say to Cosmos as he walks up the steps behind us, carrying a box of wine.'

'Is no problem,' he says. 'You lead, and I will follow.'

As soon as I start to climb, heaving the bag up while simultaneously lifting my habit to avoid standing on it and clinging onto the handrail, Cosmos stops me.

'Give to me,' he says, taking my bag in addition to the heavy box of wine. 'It's fine. I can take.'

So now he is carrying everything, and I am holding nothing, but still, I struggle up the steps. They are so steep and uneven. By the time we get halfway, the handrail stops. I never realised this on the way down, but there's nothing to hold on to. I don't notice this at first, so I lean over to grab the rail that isn't there and face plant into the dirt.

'Oh my goodness. Are you OK,' asks Cosmos.

'What the hell?' says Charlie.

'All fine. Nothing to worry about. Haven't you seen a woman in a habit with her head in the mud before?'

Once I'm upright, I hitch the thing up to my knees and stomp upstairs with all the grace of a charging rhinoceros. Carlos jogs up behind me without being remotely out of breath and without a spot of sweat on his unlined brow. Charlie is the same. She comes skipping along to me.

'Did you really just fall head-first into the flowers?'

'I kind of misjudged the handrail.'

''There was no handrail.'

'Yep - that was the root of my misjudgment.'

She hugs me, then sets off on her way.

'Follow me,' she says, leading us along the seafront. I'm still holding up my habit as I approach Cosmos to ask him whether I can take the bag of food from him.

'Oh, don't lift the skirt,' he says, his eyes full of alarm as he looks around. 'You must not lift the skirts. It is bad for people to see this. They think you are from the church.'

I'm holding it above my knee; I'm not flashing anyone.

'OK,' I say meekly. 'But it's long; it's dragging on the ground.'

I let the skirts of my habit swish back down and follow him and Charlie towards our hotel.

As soon as we get to the front, there is a massive cheer from the balcony where the girls and Juan all stand, raising their glasses as they toast our arrival with food and more wine.

'Hey there,' shouts Juan, addressing Cosmos. 'Do you want to come and join us for a drink?'

'I can't, my friend. I must work. I will see you tomorrow, yes?'

'We'll be down for breakfast,' says Juan.

'OK. Have fun.'

He hands us the food and drinks, and Juan runs down to help us carry it all up.

I watch him cast an eye over the bags packed with food.

'Ladies, you have outdone yourselves,' he says. 'Absolutely wonderful.'

'I'm afraid it's nothing to do with us,' I say. 'It was all Cosmos. He said he'd rustle up a feast for us. So we don't even know what's in here.'

On the balcony, we lay everything out and begin to examine it. 'I'm starting to regret the massive pizza,' I say to Charlie. 'I'm stuffed.'

'Don't be ridiculous...you wiped the oil off the pizza - it was calorie-free. Get stuck in, woman.'

The food is laid across tables they brought out from the room while we were at the cafe, wine is poured, and all is well with the world. 'There's just one thing we need,' says Juan, walking onto the balcony with his speaker. 'A little bit of music.'

There's a slight pause, during which Juan bashes the side of his speaker to get it to work. Then *The Sound of Music* bursts through the system, and we all sing along like lunatics.

'How do you solve a problem like Maria?' is naturally directed at Maria, while Juan sings 'Edelweiss' to me.

Then, long after most sensible-thinking people have headed for their beds, we hurl out the words to 'Climb Every Mountain' with reckless disregard for the tune.

'This, my friends,' I say, adjusting my wimple theatrically, is what you call a top-notch hen weekend.

CHAPTER 11

For the love of God, I haven't felt this bad for years. Every time I try to sit up, or even lift my head off the pillow, the banging and crashing in my skull leaves me weak and helpless. I take a long sip of water and lie back down, pulling the duvet over me. There, that's better. In minutes I have fallen into a deep, luxurious sleep in which I dream that I'm a butterfly, living in a cottage with loads of other butterflies. It's beautiful. There is a lot of food and I have butterfly friends everywhere. But when the evening comes, and I decide that I want to change back into a human, I realise that I don't know how to. I try to explain that I used to be a person called Mary Brown and I'd like to go back to being her, but the other butterflies just laugh at me, and screw up their little butterfly faces.

'Come on, lazy bones,' comes a loud cry.

I'm instantly thrown. Was that one of the butterflies? It sounds like Charlie. Perhaps she's a butterfly, too, now. Good. She can help explain to these daft red admirals that I am a human in a butterfly body.

'It's time to get up.'

'Are you a butterfly?' I ask in a sleepy voice.

'A butterfly? Have you been drinking already?'

It takes me a few seconds to adjust and remember where I am. *Oh, thank God I'm not trapped in a butterfly body. I'm on my hen weekend.*

'Are you getting up, or are we going to have to come and tip you out of bed?'

'I'm coming, I'm coming,' I say. 'Is it late? I was having such a deep sleep.'

'About butterflies, by the sound of it.'

'Yeah, something like that.'

'Well, now you must get up and act like a bride-to-be, please.'

'I ***am*** acting like a bride-to-be. I'm a bride-to-be that sleeps a lot.'

'No. We want you to be a bride-to-be that wakes up and comes out with us to have some fun,' says Charlie. 'We're not here long. We need to get going. So put on your nun's habit, and let's get some breakfast.'

'I have to do the whole nun thing again today?'

'Yep.'

'The wimple and everything.'

'The whole shebang.'

'Even in this weather?'

'Yes, of course you must do it in this weather. Nuns don't slip out of their habits and into their bikinis as soon as the sun comes out, and neither should you.'

'Great.'

Honestly, I thought this Sound of Music theme was a fabulous idea when it was first mooted because I imagined we'd all be running through the streets in habits. So far, it's only me stumbling over my skirts. Not that I mind. I'm so thrilled to be on my hen weekend that I'd wear anything they asked me to. I will happily put up with the cumbersome black material that drapes on the floor. And the wimple that makes my face look about 20 times its normal size (and my face really does look terrible without the curtain of hair swishing across it. I look like a heavily made-up puffer fish beaming out from the whiteness of the cotton).

I don't mind any of that. What disturbs me is how people's eyes drop when they see me. They look at me with a half-smile, then down as if bowing in my presence. It's as if they think I am morally superior to them. I don't like that at all. I don't like conning people into thinking I'm something I'm not. It doesn't seem right.

So, to make it very clear that I'm not a nun, but a bride-to-be on her hen weekend, I layer on more make up than usual, add pink glitter to my temples, and slip on the lacy knickers that Ted was so worried about.

I walk out onto the balcony to greet the others, smiling at Juan as he wolf-whistles at me. 'Super Sexy, sparkly nun,' he says.

'Oh yeah,' I reply. 'That's the way I roll.'

'Come on then,' says Charlie. 'Let's get this super, sparkling nun some breakfast.'

We head down to the lovely little cafe by the sea for breakfast. It involves galumphing down the stone steps of course, and Charlie makes a point of showing the others what an idiot I mad of myself when I face-planted into the ground, but once we get there, the magnificent view more than makes up for the mockery. It seems even more spectacular than last night, with shafts of light from the mid-morning sun bouncing across the gentle waves. There are sunbathers dotted across the sand below us, and windsurfers out on their boards, despite the lack of any discernible breeze.

'Heavenly,' says Veronica as we sit down at a table which catches the sun and gives us the best view of the sea. She sits back and drops her head, so her face is lifted to the sun. She sees me watching her. 'You OK, Mary?'

'Perfect,' I reply. 'Absolutely bloomin' perfect.'

'Hey, hey, hey. You are back, my lovely English friends,' says Cosmos, charging over to us with his hands in the air, and greeting us as if we were returning victorious from battle.

'How lovely that you have come back. Did you enjoy your feast last night.'

'It was so good,' I say, taking off my sunglasses. 'We loved it.'

'Oh my, you look so pretty today.' he says, seeing the pink makeup sparkling brightly on my cheeks. 'I have never seen such a beautiful nun.'

'I know you don't approve of me dressing up like this,' I say.

'Oh. It is okay for me. I no disapprove, but in this country, it is not good to joke about nuns'

'Darling, it's a tradition in England,' says Juan. 'On hen weekends, the hen must dress up. It's all good fun.'

'Come, come, I find you nice place in shade,' he says, beckoning us off to the far corner of the cafe where there's a rustic bamboo canopy over the tables, out of the sun's rays.

It looks lovely in the area he's trying to take us to, with the canopy providing shade but also privacy. Instead of chairs, there are sofas covered with brightly coloured cushions. I can see why he thinks we might enjoy it.

'No, we like it here,' says Veronica. 'We want to be in the sunshine.'

'You English are crazy,' he says. 'Completely crazy. You wanna stay here? OK, you stay there. I go get you menus.'

As he retreats, he lays his hand gently on my shoulder. 'Must be careful not to upset people,' he says. 'Dress as nun is not good here.'

I smile at him and slip on my glasses. I suppose it is an odd tradition; this need to dress up and party, perhaps they don't do that in Crete. But I know that this habit isn't going anywhere, and if I try to take it off, I will be struck down by all my fellow hens.

Ultimately, we opt for what could only be described as an untraditional Greek breakfast. A combination of tiredness and hangovers has driven us all into the jaws of carbohydrates. I'm also craving chees; Greek yoghurt with honey isn't going to cut it this morning. So I go for a lamb moussaka with fries instead of the light and healthy Mediterranean breakfast I should have. Like I say, untraditional! Oh well, it's almost 11am; this is brunch, really. And everyone knows that the rules of brunch are that you can eat what you want - lunch items, breakfast items - anything.

Once I've placed my absurd order, it opens the floodgates for the others to join me in ordering hangover-kicking food items. We've got olives, chunks of bread, loads of fries, and meaty dishes on the way. But, to be fair to Cosmos, he just writes the orders down without commenting, then smiles at us when he's finished.

'Great choices,' he says, without a hint of sarcasm. 'I will make it all for you now.'

We've managed to hit the cafe at a good time, after breakfast and lunch, so there are quite a few empty tables. This strikes me as the sort of place which is usually packed. It has everything you want from a cafe by the sea; endless views of the ocean, friendly staff, a vast menu, and these delicious smells that keep sweeping across from the kitchen on the gentlest of summer breezes.

'I'm looking forward to this,' I say. 'My need for carbs is quite big right now.'

'I hear you,' says Juan. 'I'm going to throw myself face first into my chips when they come.'

I'm thrilled to report that Juan didn't drop his face into his food, but he did make very short work of the gigantic meal that he was confronted with. I made quite a dent in mine, but couldn't finish it, which was rare for me.

'What shall we do now then?' asks Juan.

'Go back to sleep?' I suggest, but Karren is having none of it.

'No, we're not going back to the hotel; we're out to play. So what are the options?'

'We could go and chill by the pool...catch some rays and consume some cocktails.'

'Great idea,' says Charlie. 'The only slight flaw in this plan is that our hotel does not have a swimming pool.'

'Ah, yes,' says Juan. 'But I know one that does. The big hotel we drove past has a lovely pool, and according to Calista, it's such a sprawling place that no one ever asks whether you're a guest or not.

'That sounds perfect. One condition though – you have to let me take this God-forsaken habit off when we're sunbathing.'

'Of course,' says Juan.

CHAPTER 12

As we leave the cafe, Cosmos gives us a baguette and some ham to get us through the day. 'All free for you; all free,' he says as he pushes them into my arms. I'm not sure whether I really want any more food ever again. The thought of carrying this little brown paper bundle around all day is quite nauseating when I'm feeling so full that I can't breathe. It also means that I must carry it while walking up the steps which isn't ideal.

It's really very hot now and though I'm unlikely to burn with this habit on, it is becoming hideously uncomfortable inside its cumbersome blackness. I have a new and very profound respect for nuns who must wear these all the time.

'I have to get out of this thing before I die,' I says to Juan once we reach the top. 'I'm baking alive.'

'Yeah, come on, let's all go and get changed and get down to the pool.'

As we walk back to our hotel to get our swimming stuff, Juan chats about how lovely the hotel is and how much fun we will have. It does sound good, but I'm hardly listening to him; I'm so distracted by the sight of a dog curled under the shade of a tree. He's emaciated as he lies, ribs visible beneath his thin and patchy fur.

I think immediately of Elvis, my gorgeous, sweet, and loyal little puppy friend at home. I miss him. I didn't imagine missing a dog, but there's something about the way a dog will look at you…his eyes full of love and devotion. There's something about the way a dog will snuggle up to you, demanding nothing but closeness and the warmth of you. And there's the way a dog will play.

Elvis has developed this habit of dropping the ball for me to throw, then as soon as I get near the ball to throw it, he picks it back up again and trots away, little bottom and tail wiggling into the distance. I wonder when anyone played with this little dog.

'Hello,' I whisper, as I bend down, and reach out to stroke him, but he pulls back, terror in his wide eyes.

'Some food?' I ask, as if he can possibly understand me, and I pull some of the serrano ham from the brown paper package. The dog grabs the food from my hand and retreats farther under the tree. Once he's finished it, he looks up. I have already pulled another piece from my bag and he takes a tentative step closer to me and allows me to gently touch his head while he eats.

He looks so hungry I can't bear it, so I take all the ham from the bag and lay it out under the tree, watching as he buries his head and eats it all. He must have had half a dozen large slices. Next, I offer him water, tipping some of my bottled water into my hand and holding it out for him to drink.

'What on earth are you doing?' asks Juan, coming up beside me and seeing the thirsty dog. 'Get away from that mangy thing, or you'll get ill with something. He looks filthy.'

As if sensing the anger in Juan's voice, the little dog retreats, and trots away.

'He's just thirsty and starving,' I say.

'Have you been feeding him?'

'No, I just gave him water,' I lie.

'Oh good. As long as you haven't given the mongrel all of our lovely ham, I'm looking forward to eating that later.'

I look up to see the dog, still trotting off, but his tail is up. I may not have done much for him, but he's had a moment of care and happiness. Every creature deserves that.

Juan and I catch up with the others and we walk back together, arm-in-arm, singing 'Mary's Getting Married in the morning, Ding Dong the bells are going to chime…' until we reach the point where no one knows any more of the words, and we have to go back and start at the beginning again.

'Right, ten minutes to grab swimming stuff, and we meet back down in reception?' says Karren.

'Oh no, darling. I need a bit more time than that to make myself beach body ready. Half an hour?' says Juan.

'Suits me,' I say. 'I need to call mum and check on wedding stuff before we head out.'

'OK, 30 minutes it is. See you all later,' says Veronica, opting to run up the stairs instead of taking the lift. She was the only one not to order a ridiculously fattening brunch. I need to be more like Veronica. BMV: be more Veronica.

Once I'm in the lift, Maria gives me a huge hug.

'What was that for?'

'For inviting me away with your lovely friends, and for being so kind to that dog. I saw you; you gave him all the ham. Good work!'

'Thank you.'

I call mum as soon as I step out of the lift.

'Oh darling, how are you doing?' she asks. 'Are you having a lovely time? What sights have you seen?'

I don't want to tell her that we haven't done anything but

eat and drink, so I go for a very casual. 'We're having a lovely time, it's so warm here.'

'Oh, I'm glad. I was talking to Brenda from down the road. Do you remember her? Her husband used to play scrabble with your father until he left for the lady who works in the King's Head. Anyway, she says that Knossos Palace is magnificent and worth seeing, and she said that her nephew went to Heraklion Archaeological Museum and thought it was wonderful. Mind you, he's an archaeologist, so I suppose he would find it interesting. But, unfortunately, I can't remember his name now. Brian? I think it may be Brian, or is that his father? Hang on, I'll ask your dad….'

Mum's about to shout out to my dad to ask him for the name of someone I have no interest in, so I stop her in her tracks.

'It doesn't matter, mum. Honestly. It doesn't matter what the guy's name is. That's a good tip; I'll go to the archaeological museum. Everyone will be thrilled with that suggestion.'

'Yes, you could go this afternoon. Shall I check on the website to see whether they are open?'

'No, mum. I'll find out. I just wanted to check with you about the wedding arrangements. Is everything going to plan?'

'Of course it is love. Nothing to worry about at all. We'll go and pick up the dresses and the veil and shoes and everything on Monday morning. The hairdresser is coming over Monday morning to do a trial run with your hair to check you like it. I've spoken to Ted and he's been onto the venue and the caterers and there's nothing to worry about there. The menu choices you made are all fine. Ted and I are going to keep in touch and chat every day. He's such a lovely man, Mary. I've never known a man be so helpful when it comes to planning a wedding.'

'He is lovely, mum, but it's his wedding as well - it's only fair that he helps out.'

'Yes, yes. I'm just saying that you've got a good one there, Mary. Don't mess things up.'

'How do you mean? We're getting married in four days, I'm not likely to mess things up now, am I?'

As I say that, I genuinely mean it. I have no idea, as I chat away, discussing when the flowers will be arriving and who is bringing the cutlery, that I am about to get myself into such a riotous mess that I do, indeed, mess things up just a few days before the wedding.

'RIGHT, well I'd better head off mum. We're all heading out somewhere nice this afternoon.'

'Oh, where are you going?'

I glance down at my habit. 'There's a beautiful old convent, set into the rocks, we're going to look round.'

'Oh, how beautiful. What a lovely thing to do. Make sure you're covered up from head-to-toe, won't you? They don't like ankles and shoulders on show in places like that.'

'Yes, all completely covered up, mum. Don't worry.'

I spend so much time chatting to mum that I hardly have time to call Ted, but I want to speak to him after hearing how helpful he's been to mum. Unfortunately, his mobile appears to be switched off, so I grab my swimming stuff and call him on his work phone. He answers almost straight away.

'I'm coming to you live from Crete,' I say.

'Oh, heavens. I wasn't expecting it to be you. I'm just waiting for a call about the HSBC contract. Why didn't you call the mobile.'

'I did, but it's switched off. It went straight to voicemail.'

'Yes, of course it did. Sorry, I forgot to charge it up last night. I got so bloody drunk with Mike, it was ridiculous. I ended up going on a police car chase at some ungodly hour of the night.

'What are you talking about?'

I clamber into my swimming costume, throw on a lovely peacock blue and green kaftan, and leave the room, still chatting to Ted. I decide to walk down the stairs rather than take the lift. BMV, remember. Always BMV.

While I walk down, Ted regals me with the story of his evening. It all started with an early drink with Mike, which became another drink, and another, then there was a curry and so much drink he could barely stand. Then, Mike got a call. There was a significant development on an undercover international investigation he'd been working on. A guy wanted for questioning was flying into Heathrow airport. So Mike wanted to go with them to arrest the guy.

Now, the thing with Mike is that he can really hold his drink. I mean, *really* hold it. He drinks loads, all the time. It's one of the reasons I've taken against him. Whenever Ted goes out with him, he comes back in bits.

So, when the call comes in, Mike is way more sober than poor Ted, who's about to collapse. Mike perks up immediately. 'Come and pick us up from Putney High Street,' he says. 'We're in Khani Curry Palace, the Indian restaurant near the station. I have a civilian with me, but he'll be no trouble.'

'Oh my God!' I say. 'So, you ended up going on a major police investigation.'

'Yeah, then it all ended up going pear-shaped somehow. It was the wrong guy on the plane, and Interpol was involved, and Mike and his team had to fly to Athens.'

'Wow, that sounds so dramatic. What happened to you?'

'I don't really remember. I think I fell asleep in the back of the car. I texted Mike this morning and he's now in Turkey. I think they've got the guy.'

So, when you say you went on a major police investigation, what you actually did is fall asleep after drinking yourself into the ground?'

'Yes, I suppose that's true, but there was a major police investigation going on around me while I was sleeping Mike was radioing everyone and the sirens were going. All quite exciting, in a way. I feel terrible now though. Anyway, enough about me, how are you? How's it going?'

'I'm having a lot of fun. Lots of drinking and eating, and they're making me parade around the place dressed as a nun which is a bit odd.'

'Nope, that sounds ideal,' says Ted. 'I like the idea of you dressed as a nun, so no men will come on to you.'

'Darling, men very rarely come on to me. If they did, I'd just tell them I'm getting engaged to the man of my dreams next week and I am not in the least bit interested.'

'I love you,' he says, as I emerge from the stairway and walk through the reception area to the front door.

'I love you too.'

'ALL OK?' asks Juan.

'All fine. I spoke to mum, and everything is going smoothly with the wedding planning. I spoke to Ted, and he got drunk with that awful guy, Mike, last night and ended up in some mad police chase, but he slept through it.'

'This is Mike the best man?'

'Yep.'

'The one you don't like.'

'Yep.'

'Perhaps his Police chases will keep him too busy to come to the wedding. That would be good,' says Veronica.

'I would be so happy if that happened. The boys have got

their stag night tomorrow. I'm dreading finding out what trouble they get into.'

'I think Ted is way too sensible and sorted to get into any trouble. He'll just get drunk with them all and come home. If Mike chooses to end up in a gutter outside a strip club, he'll be on his own.'

'I hope you're right,' I say, hugging Veronica. She's known Ted as long as I have; we all met on a 'Fat Club' course years ago.

'He's a good man. No need to worry about him at all.'

'No, indeed,' says Juan. 'But he should be VERY worried about you, because we're going to take you off for a fantastic day of sunbathing, cocktails, and swimming. 'Have you got your swimming costume on under there?'

'I do indeed,' I say, lifting my floaty kaftan to give him a flash of my costume.

'You look very swish,' he says. 'And are they new sandals?'

'Indeed, they are,' I reply, but I'm already regretting wearing them. The ridiculous things emit fart-like sounds with every step I take.

We walk up to the corner of the road to flag down a cab, and all I can hear is the fraaaap and baaarb of my shoes.

'Oh, hello - someone's suffering after their moussaka breakfast,' says Juan. 'You OK there, Miss Farty Pants?'

'It's my sandals,' I say.

'Yeah, right,' say the others.

'Well, at least we won't lose you at the hotel,' he says, as I emit another fart sound.

We get into a cab to Hotel Cristina and are immediately reminded of our taxi from the airport, during which we sang, laughed, and ruined the work of an off-duty police officer.

'I thought he'd stay in touch,' says Charlie. 'He said he was going to take us out and show us around the town.'

'Yeah, only because he wanted Veronica to be his special friend,' I say.

'At least I made a friend.' replies Veronica. 'Unlike you losers.'

'Mary made a friend,' says Juan. 'I saw her staring lovingly at him.'

'Oh Mary, you're obviously attracting men when you wear your habit, in an 'I'm out of bounds, therefore more alluring' sort of way,' says Veronica. 'You know what men are like with their Madonna/whore thing. They see women are being pure and untouched and thus perfect to be wives and mothers, or they see them as dirty and suitable for just one thing. You, looking gorgeous while dressed as a nun - you're breaking them apart. They don't know whether to adore and nurture or shag you senseless.

'Ha, very good, Veronica, but Mary wasn't being friends with a man, she was being friends with a very mangy, skinny dog.'

'I felt sorry for him,' I say, defensively. 'He looked sad and homeless and so thirsty and hungry.'

'You're obsessed with dogs since you got Elvis,' says Juan. 'I've never known someone go from barely noticing a dog, to falling in love with them all like some sort of lunatic.'

'I think that probably applies to most people who get a dog, doesn't it?' I say. 'You don't realise how incredible they are, and how they will crawl under your skin and love you endlessly and completely until you get one. I think a lot about getting many, many more dogs.'

'No,' Juan says before I hardly finish the sentence. 'Just 'no'. You're already like some nutter, walking along the road, talking to him. We don't need you to be sleeping in a bed with 50 of them at night.'

'I have even worked out what I'd call them. For starters, I'd have corn, chili and hot.'

'They're ridiculous names.'

'No, they're not. Corn Dog, chili dog, and hotdog.'

'Ha, ha,' says Maria supportively. 'Good one.'

Juan treats her to a glare.

'And if I had a female dog, I'd call her Daisy.'

'See, now you're encouraging her,' says Juan. 'Don't encourage Mary when she's farting all over the place and talking about dogs.'

'OK. I'll bite…why Daisy?'

'I'm so glad you asked. Because when my imaginary dog is playful and funny, I'd call her Crazy Daisy; when she's sleepy, I'd call her Lazy Daisy. And when she's…um…'

'That's all you've got, isn't it?'

'No,' I say. 'When she wakes up from a sleep and is not quite with it, I'll call her 'Hazy Daisy'.'

I've really run out of ideas now.

'Oh, and when she misbehaves and I need to procure a stun gun from law enforcement agents, I'll call her 'tazy daisy.'

'Here we are.' says the taxi driver. 'Hotel Cristina. The loveliest hotel in Hersonissos.'

'Thank goodness for that,' says Juan. 'If I have to hear any more about the names Mary is planning for her imaginary dogs, I'll throw myself into the road.'

'When I'm 60, I will have dozens of cats and dogs. The house will be so full that you won't be able to get in.'

'Good. I won't want to get in if the house is full of nasty, smelly pets.'

CHAPTER 13

We step out of the taxi and walk cautiously towards the front of the hotel. There are doormen either side of a revolving door. Beyond the glass front you can see into an elegant entrance hall. This is a proper hotel, with uniformed porters running around carrying bags, shiny marble floors and glamorous pillars.

'How are we going to manage this, then?' I ask.

'We're going to style it out,' says Juan. 'Follow me.'

And so, we do. We all troop into the hotel behind Juan. He is wearing his black micro shorts with green sequins down the sides and a green vest with 'bitch' on it. To be fair, he's thrown a towel over his shoulders, so it hangs down his front, thus hiding the offensive word. The only problem is that the towel is nicked from the hotel and has 'property of Xenia Hotel' on it. It might be better that he's not yelling 'bitch' at everyone, but it's not ideal that he's screaming 'thief' instead.

Juan is followed by Veronica who looks stunning, and - to be honest - I'd have put Veronica at the front, approaching the doors first, if I were leading this assault on the hotel's facilities. There's no chance any red-blooded male would turn her away in her red bikini with a diaphanous kaftan thrown on top and cork wedges, making her already tanned and ridiculously toned legs look even longer and more shapely.

Then there's me, my nun's habit cast aside for the day, as I enjoy the feeling of the sun on my limbs. I look adorable with my kaftan of shimmering blues, oversized sunglasses, glossy lipstick, and farty sandals. Then there's Charlie and Karren, followed by Maria, who's in a little world of her own, lifting her head up to the sunshine and breathing in the fragrant air. A gentle smile plays on her lips as she enjoys the warmth, serenity, and perfume all around us.

'Morning,' says Juan, doffing an imaginary hat at the doorman as he sails past him and into the staggeringly beautiful reception area.

As was entirely predictable, the men stare longingly at Veronica as she passes by, so I move quietly in her slipstream: head in the hair, staring ahead, farty noises being emitted from my sandals as I go. I'm never buying cheap shoes ever again.

Remarkably, Juan is right. Our confidence (and Veronica's curves) mean we can stride straight through the reception area and out to the beautiful pool deck.

'Wow,' I say, looking around at the three pools in front of us. One of the pools is small, shallow, and clearly for children, with a collection of brightly coloured toys bobbing on the surface, but the other two are exactly what we're looking for. One is enormous - a large, square pool that I imagine is used for proper swimming and aqua aerobics. The other pool is kidney-bean-shaped and fringed by palm trees, eucalyptus, and thyme. There are sunbeds scattered around.

'That's the one for us,' declares Juan. 'People won't be able to see us if we're tucked in behind the palm trees.'

We march over there and all grab a sunbed, swivelling them round to face the sun.

'This is the life,' I say as I slather myself with suntan lotion. 'This is proper holiday stuff. I'm going to try and get a tan.'

'Just make sure you don't burn,' says Maria. 'You don't want a bright, red, peely face in the wedding photos.'

I pile on more sun cream because I don't want a bright, red, madly peeling face in the wedding photos.

Veronica gives a sigh of appreciation. 'These sunbeds are so soft. Who'd have thought that was possible? Hotel sunbeds are normally insufferable. I'm going to enjoy today.'

She wriggles her legs around as she gets herself comfortable. If I did that, the hotel residents would be treated to podgy white limbs that haven't seen a drop of sun all summer. But her's are just perfect. They are annoyingly long, lithe, and tanned to the prettiest shade of milky coffee.

'Put those things away; you're making me very depressed,' says Karren.

'Ha, ha! I was thinking the same,' I add.

'I don't mind one little bit,' says a voice from behind a succulent. We all look over to see a rather burly, blond man sitting to the right of us. He has a strong German accent and a wide, welcoming smile.

Veronica, Karren, Charlie, and I remove our sunglasses in one synchronised move. He's really handsome...lovely twinkly blue eyes, muscles bursting out of his chest, and the beginnings of a tan. And that gorgeous big smile could melt a female heart at 20 paces.

'Are you here on holiday?' asks Juan. I notice he's also taken his sunglasses off and is peering along with the rest of us. I don't fancy his chances much, though...our German friend has his sights firmly on Veronica.

'No. I work here. I'm a lecturer at the university.'

'In Crete?'

'Yes, based in Heraklion.'

'Blimey, that's a good gig, isn't it?' says Charlie. 'Partying on a holiday island for a few years.'

Our German friend looks a bit blank, then says he's confused about the word 'gig.'

'You know - it's a good job,' explains Veronica.

'Oh, I see. A good job. Yes. I'll remember that. Yes, very good. Not so much partying, though. Lots of work to do.'

'There are worse places to be based if you're a university lecturer,' I say. 'I'm Mary, by the way. This is Veronica, Juan, Charlie, Maria, and Karren.'

'I'm Leopold. Call me Leo,' he says, sitting up and shaking hands with us all. 'Are you here on holiday?'

'Yes, we're here for a hen weekend,' explains Veronica. 'Mary here is getting married on Tuesday.'

'On Tuesday?' he says. 'Wow, that's very soon. Congratulations.'

'Thank you.'

'That must be a lovely feeling...to have met the man you want to marry.'

'Yeah, it certainly is. I mean - I've met a few absolute lunatics along the way, but this guy - he's fab. I know he's the one.'

'Aaaahhh...' say the girls.

I look at Juan. 'Aren't you going to say ahhhh, as well?'

'No, darling, but I think Ted is fab, and the fact that you are marrying him is quite wonderful.'

'How lovely,' says Leo, genuinely moved by Juan's words. 'Mary, did you know straight away that he was the one for you?'

'Gosh, no. Ted says he knew I was the woman for him the minute he saw me, but I took a bit more time to realise that he was absolutely right.'

'When you say 'absolutely right,' what do you mean? How do you know you've met the right person?'

'I think you know deep within you. I'm so sure I'm not even questioning it for a second. Not one bit of me thinks Ted might not be the right man. He is.'

'If you're questioning it, the relationship might not be right?'

'No - I don't mean that. I suppose I'm trying to say that you should wait until you don't have one flicker of doubt before taking it further.'

As we chat, I see a beautiful woman approaching us. She's tall and skinny with a huge black, wide-brimmed hat. She looks spectacular as she approaches in her black swimming costume and matching black shoes. She walks right up to us, and it takes me a second to realise that she's with Leo. She kisses him on the cheek and settles herself on the sunbed next to him. There are sighs of disappointment, and we take this as our cue to sit back down on our loungers.

'Well, I won't be competing with that,' says Karren.

'This reminds me of Love Island,' I say. 'All these people lying around on sun loungers around a pool.'

As I say that, Veronica's phone bleeps. 'I've got a text...' she shouts, jumping to her feet. We all collapse with laughter.

'If there's a re-coupling, I'll have the German,' shouts Karren.

It all feels like the funniest thing we've ever heard as we howl with laughter, giggling and whispering to one another about how great it would be if 're-coupling' could be brought into everyday life.

The lady on the sunbed next to Leo clearly disagrees. She sits up sharply, takes off her sunglasses, and glares at us.

'I'll get us some cocktails,' says Juan. 'Mojitos all round?'

Juan doesn't wait for the answer; he doesn't need to. Instead, he just trots off to the bar and returns minutes later.

'They're bringing them over,' he says, settling on his bed.

I catch his eye as he lies down, and I give him the biggest smile in the world, which says: this is fab, you are fab. Life is great. Thanks for being part of it.

Leo's girlfriend gets up and wanders off quite frequently during our stay at the pool. Every time she disappears, Leo starts to talk to us again, telling us about his job at the university law department. But every time the lady in black returns, she glares at us and says something clearly offensive in Greek, then he rolls over and pretends he hasn't been speaking to us.

'This is crazy,' says Juan. He's just returned from the bar, having ordered our fourth afternoon drink. 'Is he forbidden from speaking to people in front of her? I wonder what's going on?'

'No bloody idea,' I say. 'It's very odd.'

Right on cue, she stands up and wanders off again. Minutes later, the barman, in his smart white outfit, comes over with his silver platter, bearing our drinks. This time, though, he's accompanied by a man in a shirt and tie.

'Excuse me, you are staying at the hotel?'

Uh-oh, here we go.

'No, we're not. We came to have some drinks, is that OK?'

'You can buy drinks at the non-residents' bar next to the reception area, but you cannot use the residents' facilities if you are not a resident.'

'Oh, sorry, we didn't realise,' says Veronica. 'We haven't used the pool or anything; we've just had drinks. We'll make sure that we use the non-residents' bar from now on.'

'I am going to have to ask you to leave the pool area,' says the manager.

'But they are with us,' says Leo. 'Lina and I are residents, and these are our friends. Is that a problem?'

The hotel manager looks stumped. He sees Lina

approaching and goes over to talk to her. Leo walks over to them, and we hear raised voices.

'I bet that bloody bitch is trying to get us thrown out,' says Juan.

'Do you think she went and told the manager?' I ask.

'Absolutely.'

'What a cow,' says Karren.

We watch the group as the chat continues. You don't have to be a body language expert to interpret Leo's mood as he throws his arms into the air and raises his voice.

'I would like these friends to stay,' says Leo, speaking English for the first time in their discussion, presumably so we can understand what's going on.

'Look, we don't want to cause any trouble,' I say. 'Leo, you are very kind, but this situation is clearly difficult. So we'll head into the bar.'

'No, please stay. This is insane.'

'They are not residents,' says Lina.

'No, we are not,' says Juan. 'We don't much like the people who stay here. Rather too dull for our tastes. Come on, let's go and get wild. You are very welcome to join us, Leo.'

'Thank you, but I will stay here. I'm very sorry for all this trouble.'

'Don't worry about it at all,' says Veronica, walking up to him and giving him a kiss on the cheek.

'What a bitch. I knew I wore this t-shirt for a reason.' says Juan when we're barely out of earshot.

'And what a weird relationship,' adds Maria. 'He was so friendly and sociable, and she's, as Juan says – she's a bitch.'

'Bat-shit crazy relationship. I hope Leo's not planning to marry her. Interesting how he asked Mary all about marriage and how you know whether you've met the right one.'

'Yeah, I could have simplified it for him if I'd realised she was his girlfriend: you haven't met the right one; dump her and go out with one of us.'

They nod in agreement as we troop off inside, following the tray of mojitos.

Once in the cool reception area, we are led to a bar up a small flight of stairs. To be fair, it's a great little bar…air-conditioned and overlooking the pool, so we can spy on Lina and Leo through Charlie's binoculars. Not that we bother to spy for too long; the drinks flow, stories are told, and food is consumed.

We even persuade the barman to put some Abba on, so we can dance and sing along (they have no Sound of Music, can you believe that? Even when we start singing the tunes, they look at us blankly).

'If you like dancing, you should come tomorrow night. Everyone welcome, big party at the hotel.'

'Really?' says Juan. 'Wow, that would be perfect.'

Juan explains that tomorrow is our last night, and we are keen to do something special to celebrate my impending nuptials.

'Of course. This is the perfect party. You must come. It will be such great fun.'

'It sounds like it will. Do we just turn up?'

'Yes, just to turn up. Is a fancy dress, but no need for dressing fancy if not want to.'

'Oh yes, we're all for dressing fancy,' says Juan. 'We'll be here, all dressed up.'

'Good,' says the barman. 'I will look forward to seeing you. You are like Adonis.'

Veronica and I glance at one another. 'Wasn't Adonis the male God of beauty or something?'

'Yeah, I think so. Our lovely Juan is being hit on.'

Juan winks at the man, and the two share a lingering smile.

'Come and dance with us,' says Juan.

'I cannot. I working.'

'Come, Christos,' shouts a man from behind the bar. 'Come now.'

The man with whom Juan had been flirting runs off behind the bar, and there is a heated exchange.

'Is that because he was flirting with you?' I ask Juan. 'The manager keeps waving his hands while talking to you.'

'God, I don't know,' says Juan. 'He's gorgeous though, isn't he?'

'Very gorgeous,' I say. 'Very pretty. Just your type, Adonis.'

By early evening, the sunbeds are emptying, and the pool attendants are out in force, sweeping across the pool deck with remarkable speed, collecting glasses, towels, and other detritus left by holidaymakers with no desire to clean up after themselves.

It's still warm but not sunny, save for a streak of sunlight etched across the patio. A few people remain by the kidney-shaped pool, determined to catch the last of the day's rays. Only one man is in the sun trap. He is a wiry, older gentleman in tiny black trunks and a fedora hat. He has his hands behind his head as he languishes, his burnished, well-oiled body glowing as the sunlight hits it.

A pale man in red shorts has arrived, and seeing only a puddle of sunlight left, he pushes his sun lounger towards it so that his bed is in the sun. He is right next to the well-oiled, Fedora man who looks up and across at the interloper, raising his hands in a 'what the hell,' sort of gesture, as if to say: 'I was here first, enjoying the peace and quiet in the late afternoon sun. So what are you doing, parking your sun-lounger right next to mine?'

But Fedora man's problems have only started because

more invaders are on the way, determined to encroach on the old man's space. This time it's a couple of tanned beauties walking along the pool area in tiny swimwear. The woman has a cascade of dark hair tumbling over her shoulders and the tiniest bikini you could imagine. It really is minuscule. The man is wearing Speedos that are very small and not in a good way. They look as if he's bought the wrong size. As if he might have inadvertently purchased them from the children's department.

They walk along the pool area as if they are strutting along a catwalk. We've all seen these people before: they expect to be treated properly and get what they want. They demand that others tolerate their selfishness. I know I'm making a lot of assumptions about this couple based on them just walking, but – let's be honest - that's the point of people-watching.

They arrive in the area with the blast of sunlight, take two of the loungers, look up at the sky, and drag them towards the warm patch. They move with such speed that for a second, I think they will crash into Fedora man and send him skidding out of the target area, like in boules.

Fedora man removes his hat and stands with his arms on his hips.

But Mr and Mrs beautiful don't care. In fact, they haven't even noticed the other two. The woman removes her bikini top, lavishly covers herself with suntan oil, and then lies back down. The couple chat loudly, laugh, and spend considerable time kissing. The men watch them in dismay, clearly not happy about sitting so close to the new arrivals, nor do they appear particularly enamoured with the overt displays of affection.

This goes on for a while, and I wonder when the amorous couple will realise that they have encroached too far and move their sunbeds away.

But no. The couple stays there.

Instead, the two men - Mr. Fedora and Mr. Red Shorts are forced to pull their sunbeds away, over to the side of the pool with no sunshine.

Victory to The Beautiful People: isn't that always the way?

THE REST of my hen group are sitting by the bar, eating the nuts, crisps, and assorted snacks in front of them while I spy on the residents.

'Are you not going to come and join us?' asks Juan. 'We're having a right old feast here.'

'I'm watching this game of sunbed chess take place on the pool deck. I'm learning a great deal about how to get what you want in life.'

Juan comes from the bar and stands beside my chair as I watch.

'Isn't that Lina? Leo's girlfriend?'

'No,' I say. 'I don't think so.'

'Yes, it is. I recognise that thick, turquoise ankle bracelet. Give me those binoculars.'

Christos stands next to us. 'Yes, that is her. She is the lady of Leo. The lady who complain about you at the pool.'

'Oh my God. That's ridiculous. The damn woman had the temerity to criticise our behaviour while she's off kissing strange men.'

'She not very nice lady, she always complain.'

'Does Leo know she's kissing other blokes when he's not looking?'

'I don't know.'

'I feel like going to his room and telling him.'

'There's no point,' says Veronica. 'Don't get involved. We're never going to see them again.'

Juan keeps looking through the binoculars. 'That man is very handsome. He has a scar on his face like he's some sort of action hero.'

We leave soon after that and spend the evening back at the cafe, dancing til the early hours before we stagger back home. The whole thing is vague. I remember 'Like A Virgin' coming on and regaling Calista with the story of the cab driver who played the music so loud that he upset the off-duty police officer, and I remember lots of dancing. Then, I remember it being time to return to the hotel, where we sat on the balcony, watching the world go by through Charlie's binoculars.

As is always the case, I start to feel hungry after a few drinks.

'I need cheese on toast,' I say. 'I must have cheese on toast. Please may I have cheddar, though? Cheddar cheese on toast.'

'No, you can't,' I hear Juan say. 'There's no cheddar in Crete, only feta cheese, and that's rubbish on toast. Why don't you go to sleep, and we'll have lots of cheese tomorrow.'

'Yes, cheese,' I say, over my shoulder, as I leave the balcony, walk back through my room, and exit into the corridor without remembering to take a key.

I've no idea where the kitchen is, but I know it's downstairs, so I get into the lift and sit down. I don't press any buttons because the array of buttons is too baffling.

I think I'll just have a nice sleep instead.

CHAPTER 14

'Has anyone seen my phone anywhere?' I say, shouting across the balcony while holding my head which hurts A LOT. 'I can't find it. Did one of you guys take it?'

I've spent about 10 minutes looking for it, but I still feel very drunk and disorientated, so my searching skills aren't the best, but I'm sure it's not there.

That's why I'm on the balcony, with my sheet wrapped around me, shouting out to my fellow hens, hoping they have seen it somewhere. Perhaps one of them took it for a joke? I don't know. That would be a pretty rubbish joke, but where is it?

Down below, Crete is coming to life very gently. People are wiping down tables at the cafe over the road, holiday-makers waft by in kaftans and flip-flops, while the locals walk past in long, study skirts, jumpers, and headscarves.

Oh my God, I feel awful. I remember being at the cafe, and I can recollect coming back here, but after that, it's all a bit vague. No - that's a lie; it's not vague; I can't remember a bloody thing. No vagueness about it. Once we get back from this hen weekend, I'm giving up the booze for good. Well, after the wedding day. No, after the honeymoon.

Below me, two joggers run down the street, swinging their arms as they power along.

'Get a car,' screams a voice next to me.

Juan has emerged from his room and is looking, frankly, dreadful. 'Why do they feel the need to taunt us with their fitness?' he asks, a note of despair in his croaky voice.

Juan's hair is standing up, his eyes have disappeared into his pale face, and he's standing like an old man, hunched over and looking troubled.

'If they can't afford cabs, they should stay at home,' I say, more to offer support to him than due to any opinions on the joggers.

'Do you remember much about last night?' I ask Juan.

'Can we go and lie on your bed and talk?' he says. 'My legs aren't really working properly at the moment.'

'Yeah, that's a first-class idea. I'm still wearing the bedclothes. This is way too early to be up and about.

'Lying down is much better,' I agree.

'Now then - what were you asking me? You've lost your phone?'

'I think so. I mean - I don't have a clue when I last used it, and it's not here on charge. I wanted to call Ted, but I can't find it anywhere.'

'I bet it's in bed. I'm always doing that. I get into bed and forget to charge it, and it sleeps in the bed next to me like a little mechanical lover. Now, get up, and let's have a look.'

I amble back onto my feet while Juan shakes the duvet out. There's no sign of my phone.

'What's this?' he asks, peeling a piece of bread off the sheet. It's covered in feta cheese. Where did this come from?'

'Oh, God. I don't know, but I'm having a flashback to

going into the hotel kitchen. There was someone there. I was in the lift. But Christ, Juan, I don't know.'

Juan is laughing quite a lot at this and taking no notice of the pain and anguish I am clearly feeling.

'This is proper hen weekend behaviour,' he says. 'I approve heartily. Do you feel ready to go downstairs, face Agata, and see whether your phone was found in the kitchen?'

'NO,' I say. 'Not yet. Let's have a bit more sleep first.'

I DON'T KNOW how long it is before we wake up again, but the sound of knocking on the bedroom door rouses us.

'I'll get it,' says Juan, all sleepy-eyed. 'It's probably Charlie.'

He ambles to the door and swings it open. Agata, the hotel manageress, is standing there. She jumps back when she sees Juan and stares down at his legs.

(I should mention that Juan is wearing a pink G-string just so you can fully appreciate the scene).

'I thought this was Mary's room?'

'Yes, it is. She's in bed.'

'In bed? With you?'

'Yes,' he says. 'Well, sort of.'

'She came for a hen weekend. She is getting married.'

'Yes,' says Juan.

'This her phone,' says Agata, very sternly, walking away while muttering under her breath.

As Juan is about to close the door, she turns back. 'Mary very drunk last night. She sleeps in lift. I find her. She tells me she goes back to bed, then I find her in kitchen, in fridge. She has no key. Is not good. I find phone in fridge. Now she in bed with you. It is worry.'

'Thank you for telling me,' he says, closing the door and turning to me.

'Well. Mary Brown. Agata is not impressed with you at all. Did you hear that? Your phone was in the fridge, you great banana.'

'Yeah, I heard. Bloody hell. And she's right, you know. It's coming back to me now. She found me in the lift. Oh God, Juan. How embarrassing is that?'

'I think it's all perfectly normal behaviour. I bet Agata finds lots of guests sleeping in the lift.'

'Yeah, right. I bet she doesn't.'

Hearing about my bad behaviour the night before prompts me to raise myself from bed.

'I should go and apologise to her.'

'Sweetheart, you're on your hen weekend. You're allowed to get drunk. You have nothing to apologise for. Can you imagine what the stag parties are like out here?'

'I know, but what must she think of me? And she clearly thought we were sleeping together.'

'We were sleeping together.'

'I know, but not like that...not in the way she's thinking.'

'Who cares what she thinks? Go and get yourself showered and ready. This is our last full day, and we're off to a party tonight.'

'If I live that long,' I say, heading into the shower while Juan sits on the edge of the bed, still chuckling to himself about my antics the night before. 'What do you fancy doing this morning?'

'I'd really like to look round the place, you know - explore the sights,' I say, as I enjoy the feeling of the shower on my face. This is not the best shower I've ever been in; it's certainly not a 'power shower.' The pipes creak as you turn the water on, and rather than cascading out of the shower head, the water arrives apologetically on your shoulder. But at least it works, so I'm not complaining.

'But we have already explored the sights,' says Juan,

clearly alarmed at my suggestion for the morning. 'I certainly explored the sight of that handsome barman in the bar last night.'

'Oh, that was funny,' I say, wrapping a tiny, thin towel around me. 'When his boss came along and told him off. That was crazy.'

Do you think I should have said something to his boss, you know – to defend the barman?'

'No, definitely not. You'd have made it worse. You did the right thing by staying out of it. Anyway, you might see them tonight at the party.'

'Mmmm…seeing Christos again would be lovely. Less so his manager. Now, come on, let's go and play.'

It's agreed, despite Juan's reservations, that because I'm the bride-to-be and thus must always be obeyed, we will kick the day off by walking along the seafront to feel the wind in our hair and the sun on our faces and have a little look at what the beautiful town has to offer. Naturally, we call into the cafe on the way past to grab coffees to drink on the walk and to tell Calista and Cosmos that we won't be in later because we'll be partying the night away at the Hotel Cristina. We promise to pop in, in the morning.

'You better!' says Cosmos. 'I will come and find you if you don't come for breakfast before your flight. Hey - to show you how much we appreciate you, breakfast will be on us.'

'Thank you so much. See you tomorrow.'

'Have fun tonight,' shouts Calista.

'COME ON THEN, what does this bloody sight-seeing involve, just looking at things?' says Juan. His shoulders have sunk forward, and he's walking like a teenager forced to go shopping with his mum.

'Yes - just look around you. It's stunning.'

'OK, we'll walk for a little while as long as we end up at the market.'

'The market. That's an excellent idea.'

'Yes, you'll love it. Loads of rubbish on sale. You'll be in your element.'

Hersonissos, the village we're staying in, is lovely. It has all the attractions of a small community; bars, restaurants, shops, and a Saturday market selling all sorts of tat that I know I'll be buying in abundance later. It also has a seafront offering a refreshing sea breeze and a variety of water sports. Clearly, none of us will be troubling the water sports instructors, but the sight of the windsurfers and little boats out on the sea, their colourful sails guiding them over the water, is joyous to watch. There's a lovely peace about this little place. The guide ropes clanking against the boats' sides, the turquoise waters twisting into white peaks as they hit the golden sand. It's all quite lovely.

'Hey, Mary, look…' says Juan. He points to a street artist sitting on an old crate at the edge of the Saturday market. 'We are so going to see this chap.'

'Let me take my habit off first.'

'Certainly not,' he says. 'The habit stays in place, the wimple stays in place, and the cross around your pretty, little neck stays in place.'

I smile and shake my head. I don't argue because he said I had a pretty little neck, and no one but Ted ever says anything like that. So I'm flattered into silence.

'Sit,' says the artist, peering at me over his little wire glasses.

While I look ahead, the rest of the hen party peers over the artist's shoulder as he makes his brush strokes. There are lots of 'ooohs...' and 'ahhs…', then some worrying laughter and a great roar of applause.

'You've finished?' I say as he smiles at me.

'Here. All finish.'

He turns the page around, and I'm stunned. He's drawn a more beautiful and colourful version of me than I could ever wish to be.

I have little pink cheeks, full, glossy, pink lips, and eyelashes so long that it looks like I could take off. Bouncy blond curls emerge from beneath the wimple, and I am clutching my crucifix with lovely hands bearing perfect, painted nails.

'Thank you so much,' I say. 'I'll keep it forever.'

He places it into a stiff brown envelope, and I put it into my shoulder bag. I really will keep it forever. I'll get it framed and put it up in the house to remember my time in this lovely place with these fab people.

We say our goodbyes to the artist and head into the belly of the market. I'm drawn immediately by the brightly coloured wigs and ludicrously large earrings on sale in a fabulous stall on the corner. Glittery eyeshadows and flashing sunglasses compete against traditional Greek leather goods, elegant handbags, and neat purses.

Next to it, there's a table of homemade tomato relishes and feta cheeses and a stall devoted entirely to humous. But I'm dragged past all of these and led to the back of the market.

'We didn't bring you to wander around buying olive chutney. We brought you here because we plan to join you tonight.'

'To join me?'

'Yes - step inside here.'

Juan leads me into a fancy dress shop. He walks up to the lady behind the counter and tells her he was the man who had phoned earlier.

'Ahhh...Juan from phone call,' she says, before disappearing into the back and emerging with three large carrier bags.

'Tonight, we are all going to be dressed as nuns.'

'Oh brilliant,' I say. 'That will be much more fun than me looking a twat on my own.'

'Ah, but you aren't going to be a nun; not tonight.'

'Oh lord, why not?'

'Because you are a nun most of the time, and tonight is fancy dress, so you will be a bride.'

With that, the shopkeeper pulls a wedding dress out of one of the bags.

'Here is dress,' she says.

It looks cheap and rigid as she shakes it into shape to cheers from my hens. There's a lot of tulle in the skirt - you know that netting that makes skirts stick out like tutus.

'Slip it on,' says Veronica, stepping forward to assist me. The dress feels horrible. The netting is coarse and scratchy, the neckline has beads missing, and the embroidery is coming away. In addition, the dress has cap sleeves, the most unflattering of all the sleeve lengths. It's as if someone has cut the sleeves at the exact point where your arm is at its fattest.

In the other carrier bags are the nuns' outfits, and while Veronica adjusts the veil on my dress, they climb into their habits. By the end of the dressing-up session, we look utterly absurd. I mean, we look ridiculous.

'Where's a good place to go for lunch?' asks Juan. He is speaking slowly, and when the lady in the shop doesn't understand him, he begins to shout. Eventually, after miming eating and drinking to the woman, she nods profusely and leads us to the door of her shop.

'This,' she says, pointing further along the road. 'Best place for fun eats.'

'Thank you very much.'

So, off we all go; I'm in an oversized, unattractive wedding dress that doesn't quite do up at the back and scrapes along the ground as I walk. The rest of the hens are dressed (very unconvincingly) as nuns. Like a carnival troupe, we dance down the road, smiling warmly at the passers-by who stare at us, unsure what to make of the rather odd collection of ne'er do wells.

The cafe we are directed to is lovely, but not a patch on CeeCee's. The waiter takes us to a table at the far side, right at the back. Unfortunately, I can't determine whether he is seating us away from everyone else lest we cause trouble or allowing us some privacy. Sadly, I have to say that I suspect the former is the case.

'Why are there so few people here? It's nearly 1pm,' says Maria.

'I was wondering that. I'll ask the waiter if he ever comes back to us. I guess that people tend to eat later here, don't they? Remember last night...people didn't come out until around 10pm. Anyway, it's better if the place is empty...more staff to attend to us, no waiting for food, and no delay between bottles of wine. Talking of which...what do you fancy? Red or white?'

I look around the table at them all. A bunch of loonies in wimples. This is so fab. I wish I could come on a hen weekend every week.

CHAPTER 15

The waiter comes over to the table and stands sternly, looking down at his notebook. I'm unsure what we've done to upset him, but he's not engaging with us.

'Isn't usually busier than this,' asks Juan.

'Yes, busy is every day but not today. Today is quiet.'

'Why is that? Because it's Saturday?'

'Ah, no. No. Is quiet because is George Clooney day. People is watching George Clooney.'

'Oh, I see. Does Clooney have a new film out?'

'No, no. Seaside. He in the boat doing film.'

'Wait, hang on. Did you say George Clooney is out there, in a boat?'

I fling my arm seaward as I speak.

'Yes, he there.' The waiter points towards the sea. 'What would you liking to drink?'

As ever, we're torn in half over what wine to have. Half of us want white, the other half want red.

'Two bottles of each,' says Juan, which sets the day's tone.

The waiter nods and disappears into the kitchen.

'Oh, we must find George Clooney. That would be amazing,' I say. 'Let's go looking for him.'

'We can't all go, or we'll scare the man off. So let's organise a shift system,' says Juan. 'I'm very happy to lead the first party.'

Juan's on his feet and heading towards the water. 'You should come, Mary. It's your hen weekend.'

'OK,' I say, rising and indicating to Veronica that she should come too. Charlie glares at me as I give Veronica the nod. Charlie is my best friend in all the world and the one I would ordinarily invite to a potential meeting with George Clooney (when I say 'ordinarily,' that's a bit of a misnomer because ordinarily,' I don't go around meeting stars). But Veronica looked so eye-catching this morning in her red cropped halter neck top and her matching long red skirt. She's got the habit on top now, but I'm sure I can persuade her to take that off. In her red coordinates, she looks exactly the sort of woman that would catch the eye of a film star.

Yes, dear readers, I'm using her curves and tiny waist as bait. She'll attract attention, and I'll be there, in her slipstream, creeping behind her, unseen. Ninja-hen. George will invite her onto his private yacht, and before he's had time to ask her what her name is, he'll realise that I'm standing there too, and there'll be nothing George can do but ask me my name because he's bound to be too polite to chuck me off.

Anyway, that's my plan. The first step is to find out whether George is here and - if so - where.

By the time Veronica and I make it to the beach, Juan has his habit hitched up to his waist and is charging through the water. He's wading towards the very glamorous yachts.

'Is that where he is?' I shout over.

'I think he must be. They're the most extravagant boats on the water.'

While Juan continues to battle through the water,

Veronica and I join the small crowd of (mainly women) on the sand and ask in our best Greek (!) whether they know where George Clooney is.

'He there...' one of them says, pointing to a row of tiny, terraced houses.

'No, George Clooney, the actor. He's on the water in a boat.'

'No water. He there.'

The woman pulls out her phone and shows me a newspaper article. It shows Clooney standing outside one of the houses she's pointing to.

'Thank you, thank you,' I say, pulling Veronica with me as we walk over to the houses. There's no security, no sign of cameras, nothing. He can't be in there, surely.

I look to the sea and spot Juan at the yacht's mooring. He is clinging to a buoy while shouting to the guys on board.

There's no way I can shout loud enough for him to hear, so Veronica and I proceed without him. We spot that the door to one of the cottages is open and walk gingerly inside.

'George are you there?' says Veronica.

'In here,' comes a female voice.

We follow the voice through the house.

'We're looking for George Clooney,' says Veronica.

'Just through here, George,' comes the reply.

So, we walk further. These houses are much bigger inside than they appear to be from the outside. It's like a warren of corridors and tiny side rooms.

In front of us is a woman sitting on a small wooden chair, wearing a long floral house coat that swishes out around her, all over the wooden floor. Beneath it, she's wearing what looks like an old-fashioned nightdress with piles of grubby-looking necklaces. The whole look screams: 'gypsy.' On her face, she has a lot of makeup, and it's starting to run, so she resembles a freshly-painted china doll that has been left out in the rain.

'Are you looking for George?' she says. 'Did you hear that he was here and come in your wedding dress to marry him? You've even bought a vicar with you, look.'

'I'm on my hen weekend,' I say.

'Well, well.'

'Is he here?' I try. 'We're from England and would love to meet him.'

'I am from England as well,' she replies. 'I can tell your futures.'

I had a very unfortunate entanglement with a psychic once; I won't be doing that again.

'We're OK, thanks,' I say.

'Don't dress as nuns, she replies, tugging at Veronica's habit. 'Take this off. Or serve your time.'

'Thanks for the advice. We're leaving now. You don't know where George Clooney is, do you?'

'I am his personal psychic. I know where he is. I'm part of his entourage. He's based in the cottage two doors down. Those people waiting to see him on the water are wasting their time. If you really want to see him, he's two doors down. Thank you.'

We nod and rush out of the house.

'Do you think she's right that he's two doors down?' says Veronica.

'She says she's his personal psychic, so I guess she's right.'

'But she's obviously nuts. There's no way she's his personal anything.'

'Yeah, I don't know.'

'I suppose we could just go and see? There's no harm in that, is there?' says Veronica.

'It would be cool to go back from the hen weekend and tell everyone that we met George Clooney, don't you think?'

'I think that would be magnificent. We could tell everyone that though... there's no need for us to actually find him, is there?'

'That's a good point, but it would be great to have a selfie. Come on; what's the worst thing that could happen?'

Veronica doesn't reply to this, and I'm glad. The truth is that a whole lot of worst things could happen.

Two doors down, the door is ajar. Again, there's no sign of any security, so we gently push the door, and when it opens, we step gingerly inside. This house has a very different feel from the last one... it's very modern-looking and elegant, not at all cluttered, with whitewashed walls and simple grey sofas; there are no signs that anyone lives here besides a brown leather jacket thrown across the sofa.

'Hello,' says Veronica. 'Anyone here.'

There's a sound from the back of the house, and a rather muscular, not unattractive, man appears.

'Who are you?' he asks in a strong American accent.

'Hi, we're looking for George Clooney.'

'Are you crew?'

We're two English women dressed as a nun and a bride. On what planet would we be part of the crew?

'Yes, part of the crew,' says Veronica, unconvincingly. 'We have a message for the director.'

'You can give it to me,' says the man (he has 'Bud' tattooed on his massive biceps, so I suspect that's his name).

'We were told to hand it to Mr. Clooney himself.'

'George, can you come here?' shouts Bud.

We hear footsteps, then in walks the world-famous actor. He's wearing a black polo shirt, jeans, and sunglasses on his head. And he looks more gorgeous in the flesh than he does on TV. Let that sink in for a minute... more gorgeous. Can you imagine such a thing?

'Can I help you?' he asks.

He doesn't sound all that friendly, to be honest. He looks like a man who was busy working and has now been interrupted by two mad English women in fancy dress.

'They have an important message to give directly to you.'

'Go on,' he says.

'There's no message. We just want a photo with you,' says Veronica. 'I beg you. It's her hen weekend, and we're desperate. And - I'm sorry, but...'

'Ah, you're on a hen weekend. You English girls like your dressing up on hen weekends, don't you?'

'Yes,' says Veronica. 'It's kind of a tradition. We thought it would be amazing to go home with a photo of us with you.'

'Bruce - take a picture, would you.'

The man who was Bud but is now Bruce (I hope you're keeping up) takes the phone while Veronica and I fold into George's arms. Bruce snaps away while we pose like lunatics. I stick my tongue into his ear, ruffle his manly hair, and lift my leg up, so it's around his waist.

'OK, enough,' shouts the king of the screen. 'Let's leave it there. Bruce will show you out.'

I blow George a kiss and head for the front door, followed closely by Bruce. There are no heartfelt goodbyes when we reach the street, just the sound of the door slamming behind us.

To be honest, though - neither of us cares. I have no idea how we managed that, but we just met George Clooney and had our photos taken with him.

We skip back to the cafe, screaming with excitement, thrilled beyond all imagination that our campaign to meet George was so staggeringly and unexpectedly successful.

'I can't wait to see all their faces when we tell them,' says Veronica. 'I mean, really, that was ridiculous, wasn't it? George Clooney! We just met bloody George Clooney, for God's sake. George Clooney.'

'And he was beautiful. My God - wasn't he beautiful?'

'Heavenly,' confirms Veronica. 'Just stunning.'

We approach the table, ready to show everyone the fantastic pictures and tell them our wonderful tale, but the girls have news for us.

'Come here, come here,' shout Charlie, Karren, and Maria, as soon as they see us. 'Come quickly.'

'Look at this...' Charlie holds the binoculars up to her eyes. 'He's only climbing on board the bloody boat.'

She passes the binoculars to me, and I see Juan with one leg hooked over the side of the yacht, pulling himself on board. He seems so tiny up against the side of the massive boat.

'How the hell has he managed that?' I ask, genuinely baffled. Yachts are massive things.

'Oh, it's been quite a sight; he was clinging onto the buoy, then he jumped up onto the RIB next to the pontoon and stood right on the front part, where the engine is, then somehow climbed up those ropes at the side. It's been like watching an action movie about a nun who goes completely rogue and decides to steal a yacht. If George sees this, he'll sign him up for his next movie.'

'That's impressive. Juan's very flexible, though, and surprisingly strong. If I tried to climb aboard like that, I'd sink the boat.'

'Oh, behave. You weigh hardly anything these days.'

'Yeah, tell that to the women who run wedding dress shops.'

'They're all idiots and should be shot.'

'Oh my God. Oh no. It's really kicking off here…security has spotted Juan. Shit, they don't look at all happy.'

Veronica grabs the binoculars off me and watches the drama unfold for herself.

'He's being lifted over. Oh blimey, he's waving his arms

around - you know, that way he flings his arms about when he's worried or angry about something. Well, he's doing that. Now he's being escorted across the boat.'

'I hope he's OK. Poor thing,' says Maria. 'What possessed him to try and climb aboard a yacht, for heaven's sake?'

'George Clooney,' say Karren and Charlie in unison.

'And look on the bright side - there's every chance he's going to meet him,' says Karren. 'George is bound to come out of his cabin to see all the fuss.'

Veronica puts the binoculars down and looks at me.

'There's something we haven't told you. You distracted us with all this talk of Juan spidermanning his way up the boat in a nun's habit and didn't give us the chance to share our stunning news with you.'

'What haven't you told us? And pass me the binoculars.'

'We saw George Clooney.'

'Yeah, OK. Right.'

'No, honestly, we did. We met this fortune teller-style woman in a floral housecoat, and she told us not to dress as nuns and told us exactly where George was.'

'Prove it,' they say.

Veronica pulls out her phone and shows them the pictures.

There's silence. Absolute silence.

Then, quietly and very slowly, Charlie whispers. 'You have your tongue in George Clooney's ear.'

CHAPTER 16

'Still shocked,' says Charlie, shaking her head almost two hours later. 'You're not winding us up, are you? You definitely saw him.'

'Yes,' I say for what feels like the millionth time. 'I showed you all the pictures.'

'I know, but you could have doctored them or something. I don't know. I mean...George Clooney!'

'I can't quite believe it either. We just walked right in and asked to see him. There was an aggressive-looking bouncer there, but it was quite easy to persuade him to call George for us.'

'If you'd been blokes, you'd probably have been wrestled to the group,' says Karren. 'Probably helped that you were dressed like lunatics as well. Perhaps they thought you were part of the cast?'

'Yeah, I think he believed that we were something to do with the filming.'

Juan is listening in silence as water drips from the end of his nose, and he mops his face for the hundredth time.

'I made a terrible decision there, didn't I?'

He has been very somber since we rescued him from the security people on the boat and persuaded them not to call the police.

'They were so bloody unreasonable.' he says. 'I tried to explain, but they kept going on about keeping my mouth shut and telling me they would tie my arms and legs together and throw me in the water if I said a word about what I'd seen on the boat.

'I swear to God, I saw nothing on the boat. I was on it for about five minutes and shoved into a side room with a pile of boxes and parcels. There was NOTHING to see. I don't know what they were talking about.'

'Probably confidential film stuff?' I venture. 'Perhaps they were worried about you leaking details of the film?'

'Yeah, probably. But does that really qualify for having my arms and legs tied up and thrown into the sea? Bunch of thugs and gangsters if you ask me. Thanks for coming to rescue me.'

'A great pleasure,' I say.

BY 8PM THAT EVENING, all thoughts of gangsters on boats have been erased from our minds as we walk into Hotel Cristina and prepare to party. Charlie is still obsessing about Clooney, of course. But I imagine we'll be obsessing about that man for the rest of our lives.

'Is he really as gorgeous in the flesh as he looks on television?'

We're both a little tipsy, wearing high heels on uneven, cobbled streets and struggling with our long dresses (her habit and my wedding dress), which reach down to the ground, forcing us to stumble and stagger even more.

'He's got this incredible smile that lights up his face. And even though he wasn't particularly pleased to see us, he still had this little twinkle in his eye. So that was very appealing.'

'Oh, I'm so cross I didn't meet him,' says Charlie. 'I should have jumped up and come with you.'

'Yes, you should have. I don't know what I was thinking. I just didn't want to leave Karren and Maria on their own because they didn't really know each other. I thought if you stayed with them, at least they would have some fun. I'm sorry.'

I can't tell her I took Veronica instead because she's gorgeous, and I thought she might help open a few doors.

We get to the hotel, and Charlie is still full of questions. I'm struggling to hear her over the loud music blaring out. The tables have been pushed back, and dancing is taking place. 80s tunes are warbling through the system as we try to hear each other.

Karren heads to the bar with the kitty and returns with mojitos, the drink of the hen weekend. We raise our glasses, shout 'cheers,' and delight in the gorgeous minty taste.

Then *Come on, Eileen* bursts across the sound system, and the drinks are forgotten as we all jump up and head for the dance floor, stomping away to the beat and singing our hearts out.

Everyone is in fancy dress, which is excellent. I have spent two days avoiding odd glances or smiling and bowing slightly, clutching my cross when the occasion demanded it. Here tonight, we don't stand out as being ridiculous. Well, I might with my wedding dress over my nun's habit. But we certainly don't look like the oddest people in the room.

A group that's arrived dressed like characters from Star Wars, including Chewbacca, whose dance moves are pretty extraordinary.

'Time to join the nunnery,' says Juan, persuading me to tear off the wedding dress in the middle of the dance floor and reveal my nun's habit underneath. It's quite a relief. Even though this place is air-conditioned, it's boiling with two big dressed on top of one another.

As I wriggle out of the dress, everyone claps as if I'm doing a striptease.

I bow at the end and bless them all.

'Fancy a drink?' says Veronica.

'Yeah, I'd actually love a glass of water.'

'A what?'

'A nice, cool glass of water.'

'So, a nice cool glass of water and a Mojito coming up.'

While Veronica and I go to the bar, the others retire, exhausted and sweaty, to the balcony seats, overlooking everyone.

'We'll bring them up,' I shout over and am treated to a thumbs up from Juan.

Veronica stands at the bar, statuesque in her wedge-heeled shoes. She must be almost six feet tall with those high heels on. She adjusts her wimple and explains to the barman that we would like a jug of Mojito. He tells her he can let her have a goldfish bowl of Mojito with six straws.

Next to her stands a short, incredibly well-dressed man. He can't be any taller than 5'2' as he stares up at Veronica lustfully.

'I love you,' he says in a strong South African accent.

'Yeah, OK,' she replies, barely glancing at him from her superior height.

'I'm going to fuck you,' he shouts out.

'Yeah, and if I find out about it, I'll be very cross,' she shouts back, leaving the bar with her massive goldfish bowl and making her way back to me.

'Best response ever,' I say. 'Best response ever.'

We join the others on the balcony. It's much less noisy, but still very crowded. People have draped their things over the table that Juan has appropriated. I push all the belongings to one side, putting down the big bowl of joy.

'Wow!' says Juan. 'That's extraordinary. Why didn't they give me one of those when I went to the bar?'

'No idea, love. I asked for a jug, and the barman suggested a fishbowl. Perfect, eh?'

'I'm just going to the loo before I get stuck into that,' I say, grabbing my handbag and staggering off toward the ladies toilets. I'm swaying as I go. What a bloody brilliant evening. What a fantastic hen weekend. It's been nuts. I even met bloody George Clooney. Who would have thought that would happen?

Happily, there's no massive queue at the ladies', so I head straight in, then walk over to the mirror.

My God, I look rough. I look washed out, and my eyes have disappeared into the back of my head. I need makeup and fast. I open my bag, pull out my lipstick, and put it on, looking at my reflection. I look worse now than before. What possessed me to buy this very dark plum shade? It looks ridiculous on me. I apply a little more, but it's even more hideous. The more I put on, the more I look like Morticia Addams. I reach in and pull out my foundation. I need to brighten my skin up a bit. I can hardly stand up as I sway in front of the mirror, rubbing the foundation into my skin. I look crazy now. What is this? It looks nothing like my foundation. Why doesn't this look like my foundation? Why do I look so terrible? Perhaps it's the lights in here? Or the unflattering outfit. I put another blob on my nose and rub it in, adding a little more, but it doesn't seem to make me look better; I look like a clown. I might just leave it there. I drop the makeup into the bag and head back to see my friends.

'Good Lord, what have you done to your face?' asks Juan when I approach.

'Heavens above,' says Karren. 'That's a very different look for you.'

'I can't do makeup when I'm drunk. Too hard,' I say, and I flop into my seat.

A minute later, a tall, elegant, dark-skinned lady walks over and takes my handbag off the table.

'Excuse me,' she says. 'This is mine.'

I look at her. She has beautiful, flawless skin and is wearing dark plum lipstick.

'Oh God, I'm so sorry,' I said. 'Your bag looks like mine.'

'Sure,' she says, taking the bag and walking off into the distance. I watch her join a group of friends, and they all look over. Clearly, she's telling them about the weird woman dressed in a habit who took her bag off to the loos.

Then I notice one of the women in the group; she looks familiar. Oh God, it's that Lina woman from the pool earlier.

'Well, that explains the mad makeup,' says Juan, raising his glass. 'Here's to women who don't recognise their own handbags.'

'Hooray!' we all shout, raising glasses and knocking back our drinks.

When I look back around, Lina is still staring in our direction. What is her problem with us?

Down below, on the dance floor, the Birdie Song is playing, and the absurd but familiar tune has us all wiggling in our seats.

'Shall we go for one more dance before we go?' says Maria.

One by one, we stand up and walk to the balcony to peer over at everyone. Dozens of different cartoony characters go through the ridiculous dance, flapping their wings and wiggling their hips.

'I wanna take my habit off,' says Karren, moving to remove the garment.

She lifts it up and over her head, forgetting that she has nothing but the tinniest g-string underneath.

'Oh shit,' she says, dropping the habit back down. 'I forgot I had nothing on.'

Down below, everyone is cheering and shouting. 'More, more, more…'

'Come on, let's give them a show,' says Juan, standing next to Karren. 'One final gesture of fun and freedom before we head back to England, and Mary ties the knot. Let's make it a hen weekend we'll remember for the rest of our lives. What do you say?'

'OK,' I say, caught up in the silliness and wildness of the moment. 'On the count of three, but we must never mention this to anyone.'

We all vow 'Don't Mention The Hen Weekend' before I count to three, and we lift the front of our habits right over our heads, squealing before dropping them back down again.

There are roars of appreciation from down below.

'And bottoms,' says Juan, so we spin around, fling our habits up, and wiggle our bottoms at the crowd below. 'I think they want to see some real bottom,' says Juan, getting too much into the whole spirit of the thing. He drops his boxer shorts and wiggles his bottom along with the birdie song before turning to face them.

'What's the matter with you all?' he shouts. 'Have you never seen a nun's willy before?'

The rest of us howl with laughter before returning to our seats and tucking into the fishbowl.

'That was crazy,' says Charlie. 'We've had a bloody good time, haven't we? Best hen weekend ever!'

'Best ever!' I reply. 'But we should never mention it.'

'Never!' says Juan.

'Let's go back to CeeCees to see the guys for a nightcap,' I say. 'I can't dance anymore. What do you think?'

There's universal agreement that CeeCee's is the way forward, so I pull out my phone to text Calista, telling her we're on our way. Everything's getting a bit blurry by this stage. Nothing makes much sense. I lean my elbow against the arm of the chair, and it slides off, so I crash down. I hear the others laughing, but this is quite comfy, with my head resting against the soft velvet armrest.

'Come on, let's go,' I hear Veronica saying. 'Let's get you in a cab.'

'I'm fine,' I say, but when I stand up, my legs don't work correctly, and my knees sort of buckle. I am caught by Veronica and Juan, who make quite a performance of helping me that I realise they're drunk too. We're all drunk. Of course we are. Why would we stand on the balcony flashing at all the people below if we were sober?

'Shall we flash one more time?' says Juan as we head towards the stairs.

'No!' says Veronica. She's trying to hold me up with one arm while holding her head with the other.

'What's wrong with your head?' I hear Karren say, though everything is so blurry and confused now, I don't know what's happening.

'We were leaning against the DJ booth for a picture. I didn't realise it was left unlocked. I fell arse over tit through it. Embarrassing.'

'That's nothing. One time I was so drunk that I walked into a fish and chip shop, grabbed a fish, and then ran for my life. I threw the fish into the river, and shouted 'swim free, little fish, swim free...' says Maria.

'That's a marvellous thing you did there, young Maria. Freeing a fish is a fine thing.'

'But it was freshly cooked in batter,' she says. 'I'm not convinced that I saved it.'

'Of course you did. You are a fish saver.'

OUTSIDE IT'S PRETTY COOL. Nothing like as cold as it would be in England this time of year, coming out of a party at 1am, but we all instinctively pull our arms around us and snuggle into our habits as three men approach the party, dressed as police officers.

'Good evening,' one of them says to me.

'Good evening,' I reply. 'Are you coming to the party?'

'No, we're not here for the party.'

'Well, that's a shame because I can heartily recommend it,' says Juan. 'If you want to see Chewbacca dancing to classics from the early 80s or witness Yogi Bear doing the Birdie Song, this is the place for you. There are a few people there dressed as sexy policewomen, so you'll fit right in.'

I notice that the officers have moved around us as Juan has been talking. We're surrounded.

'I'm going to have to ask you to come with us to the station,'

'Hahaha,' says Veronica. 'Very good. You could almost pass for real policemen.'

'We are real policemen and need you to come to the station with us for questioning.'

The man looks very Greek and stern, but his English is immaculate.

I look behind and see two of the hotel's bouncers standing behind us. We're surrounded.

'You've got the wrong people,' I say. 'We've done nothing wrong.'

'You have disgraced our religion and upset the people at the hotel.'

'We didn't upset anyone; we were all having fun.'

'Someone called to complain about your actions tonight. They say you entered the hotel illegally during the day; now you offend our people, religion, and customs. You will be arrested if you do not get into the cars.'

We stand there, dumbfounded.

'We are arresting you for scandal and misrepresentation of a costume or uniform,' says the officer. 'Into the police cars, now.'

CHAPTER 17

It would be fair to say that none of us wants to get into the police car. We continue to stand there while the police tell us that they will handcuff us and force us to come with them if we don't get in.

'I'm not getting into the car without my lawyer present.'

I know nothing about Greek law, but I watch a lot of true crime documentaries, and the right to a lawyer is always a big deal on them.

'There's nothing your lawyer can do to prevent you from being arrested. However, if you want a lawyer, we can arrange for one to come to the station.'

'But I don't understand what this is all about... What have we done that's so terrible?'

'I have told you verbally, and the details of your arrest will also be given to you in writing,' says the officer. 'Now you must come to the police station with us.'

'I'm sorry. I think there must be a misunderstanding,' says Veronica, smiling at the officer in a manner that could only be described as flirtatious. 'We had no desire to offend anyone. We were having fun because my friend is due to get married. If we promise to go back to our hotel and never wear these outfits again, would you be able to let us off? Just this once? We're leaving the country tomorrow.'

'Is no good,' says the police officer.

'We didn't mean to cause offence. I promise you. Come on...let me buy you a drink.'

'No. Is not allowed. Drinking on duty cannot be. Come...'

He must be the only man in Greece who is immune to the charms of my gorgeous, curvy friend.

Quite a crowd has developed now. Revellers leave the dance floor and come outside to see what's happening.

'I think we'll have to go with the Police,' I say. 'Or they'll get all heavy-handed and say we were resisting arrest or something.'

'I guess,' says Charlie. 'Or do we just stand our ground here hoping they get called away to another job.'

'I am asking you one final time to enter the police cars, or we will be forced to put you in there.'

'OK,' I say. Maria is sobbing beside me and, presumably, wondering why she ever befriended me in the park. It's one thing to make a friend while running around with your puppies, quite another to go on that friend's hen weekend and find yourself arrested in a foreign country in the early morning hours.

We are led to the police cars on the side of the road. The cars are white BMWs with a sleek royal blue stripe down the side. The stripe is the same colour as my big PE knickers that Ted is so fond of. How about that? I don't share that information with the officers. No doubt that will be another crime. At least I'm wearing them, though, thank God.

'Where can we get a lawyer from?' asks Juan. Despite our drunken state, we are all beginning to realise this is a huge deal.

'What?' asks the officer, spinning round. 'You are men?'

'No, we chorus. 'Just Juan.'

'I am a man,' says Juan.

'But you have lady paint.'

'I have makeup on because Mary is getting married.'

'In England, men wear makeup for a marriage.'

'Yes,' says Juan, eager to make it look like he is fulfilling a custom's demands rather than being drunk and rebellious. 'We were just having some fun.'

The driver looks over at the officer next to him and mutters a word in Greek. We have no way of translating it, but we understand it entirely. We're not behaving correctly. We're drunk and silly and dressed up, and now it turns out that one of the women is a man.

I don't know how to convey to the officers that this is all harmless fun and that we'd be very keen to apologise if we've offended anyone. We don't mean to cause offense. But every effort I make to give him my speech results in him shaking his head and looking at me as if I were a wild animal who'd just bitten him. I don't think it helps that I have very dark makeup applied patchily all over my face and am grinning at him with dark plum lips and plum-stained teeth.

'I know a lawyer?' blurts Karren. 'I've been wracking my brain and just remembered that my ex-boyfriend is a solicitor.'

'Is he a proper criminal lawyer.' asks Veronica

'Christ, I don't know. I know he was training to be a lawyer when we went out together, and now he's a fully-fledged, proper lawyer.'

'Can we call him?' I ask, trying to hide the note of desperation that has crept into my voice. 'I mean - any lawyer would do at this point, surely. If he's not the right sort of lawyer, he might know someone who is.'

The crowd of people grows as time passes. There can't be anyone left on the dance floor now. Then another police car arrives, lights flashing and sirens blazing as if he were heading to a murder scene.

The car screeches to a halt, and a devastatingly handsome man jumps out and walks over to his colleagues like a cowboy who just climbed off his horse.

Then the handsome man turns to us all.

'Do you understand why you are being arrested?'

'Yes,' I say. But...'

'Halt!' comes a cry from the hotel. 'Stop now.'

'It's Leo!' says Karren, as the large German runs across the hotel forecourt to us like a hero in a Jane Austen novel.

He shouts something in Greek, which persuades the officers to stop in their tracks. His mastery of the Greek language is spectacular. He points at their notebooks and waves his arms around. Then, finally, he stops talking and turns to us.

'I'm a law professor at the university,' he says. 'I'm not a lawyer, but I know the law.'

'Oh, my God, I forgot you were in the law department. Thank you, thank you, thank you,' I say. 'Please will you tell them that we didn't mean any harm? Lots of people dress up for hen weekends in the UK.'

'I have tried to explain to them that your actions were harmless, but they said you stripped off while wearing habits. That is not acceptable here. There was a formal complaint from a resident at the hotel, so they must take you into the station.'

'Can you come with us?'

'No, I can't. You need a proper lawyer to help you. They are taking you to the central police station in Heraklion. I will arrange for a lawyer to meet you there tonight. You also need to contact the British Embassy in Crete. Someone from the consulate will need to be involved.

'The British Embassy? Wow, is it that serious? We weren't doing anything wrong?'

'Technically, you were.'

'What? By dressing up?'

'By flashing and behaving disrespectfully. Crete is a very religious country. The crime you have committed is scandal and misrepresentation of a costume or uniform. It is a public-limited charge, so dependent on someone saying they were offended. Which they have.'

'So, what will happen now?'

You will most likely be asked to go to the courthouse, and they will see whether anyone turns up to confirm that they were offended. If no one comes, you will be freed.'

'But I can't go to the courthouse. Our flight home is tomorrow. I am getting married on Tuesday.'

Leo smiles and hugs me. 'We're going to support you as much as possible. Go with the officers, and I'll make sure a lawyer comes to the station.'

We arrive at the police station 20 minutes later and are taken into a detention room. Various officers come in and out, mainly looking at us all, sitting in our habits. We can hear the officers talking in Greek all around us, but few have even the most basic grasp of English. The guys who brought us in here seem to have disappeared. No one seems willing to explain to us what will happen next.

Karren stands up and strides towards the door, knocking gently and endeavouring to explain, in broken English, that we need a lawyer. It's incredible how speaking to foreigners who don't speak English seems to lead to a complete unravelling of one's grasp of the language. The usually calm, collected, erudite Karren is gesticulating wildly.

'We need a lawyer. Lawyers need us NOW.'

But after having appeared to understand us, they have all left the room, which is a little disconcerting. I thought their understanding would be followed by the police allowing us to call a lawyer.

It's 20 minutes before they come back into the room, accompanied by a big, stocky man who looks like he might be British. He has a mop of blond hair, not unlike Boris Johnson's, and his suits are about two sizes too large and a couple of inches too short.

The officers turn to leave, and I notice that one has a scar on his face. That's not the man Lina was with at the pool, is it? Have we been wholly stitched up? Or has the heady combination of alcohol, fear, and confusion led me to hallucinate?

'Hallo,' he says. 'I am your lawyer. I speak English, so there is no need for an interpreter, but if you want one, one can be provided for you.'

He has a strong German accent, but he speaks English well. We look at one another, unsure what to answer.

Eventually, Karren speaks: 'We're in a little bit of a pickle,' she says. 'We're here for my friend Mary's pre-wedding party. Let me tell you what happened.'

Pre-wedding party is a good phrase. It sounds less threatening than hen weekend. I'm sure that as soon as the judge hears 'they were on a hen weekend,' he shouts 'guilty,' and that's the end. But 'pre-wedding' - that's a whole different thing.

'OK, my name is Gunther. I am German, but I live in Crete and am a lawyer. Leo asked me to come and see you. Do you understand what is happening?'

'Well, we know we've been arrested, but we don't know why. I mean - we don't understand what we've done that's so awful.'

'Well, in Crete, there is a charge called: scandal and misrepresentation of a costume or uniform. This is levelled at you because you were behaving in a manner unbecoming to the outfits you were wearing, so you are seen as misrepresenting them or bringing them into disrepute.'

Gunther goes on to explain that he has seen cases like this before. 'It's usually stag parties who find themselves in this situation,' he adds. He tells us that people can come to the courthouse to speak out if they think we have brought religion into disrepute. If no one turns up to complain, we will be OK to go. However, if people turn up in their droves, we're in big trouble.

'People aren't going to turn up in droves,' I say. 'We haven't offended anyone.'

'Well, no, you'd think not. But Leon said that someone contacted the police about you tonight, and whoever that was is bound to turn up - so that's one person for a start. The locals here hate hen parties turning up and getting drunk, so the court notification may drag a few other people out.'

'But, we're supposed to be going home tomorrow. So, we'll have to change our flights,' I say.

'Yes, you will.'

'Oh, God. This is a nightmare. I'm getting married on Tuesday, and my dress fitting is Monday morning.'

I regret to say that I burst into tears at that point. I'm usually a tough old thing, but marrying Ted means so much to me, and we're putting this wedding together in such a short amount of time that losing time just before we say 'I do is awful. I also feel cross because we didn't really do anything wrong. Well, I suppose flashing at everyone wasn't ideal, but every stag party in the history of marriage does that. Is it so wrong? Clearly, we shouldn't have worn the nuns' outfits. It was so stupid of us to wear them. Especially when we were warned that people would take offence. I just didn't think for a second that they would. I certainly didn't think anyone would ring the police. I bet it was Lina.

'Why can't they hold the court session tomorrow?' I ask.

'Because it's Sunday, and this is a religious island. Hence why they are so cross about you dressing up as nuns.'

'Have they ever watched the Sound of Music, though? Do they understand why we are dressed like this? We're dressed like the people in the musical.'

'No, I didn't go into that,' says Gunther.

'Please try,' I say. 'I know it's not much of a defence, but I think any defence is better than none right now.'

'OK, I will mention it,' he says, but we can all see that he's not convinced it will make a difference.

'This will go to court now, and if no one comes to complain that your behaviour was offensive, they will let you off, but if you don't go to court, or you object or cause a scene, the police will come down hard on you. They take this sort of thing very seriously.'

'But my flight...'

'There will be no flight home. You will go to court, and the court will decide what happens to you. If you need to make phone calls, you have the right to do that.'

'I'll make calls when they let us out of here. Do you know when that will be?'

'Not tonight. You will be staying in the police cells tonight.'

'What? Do we have to stay here? Like we're criminals?'

'Yes.'

'This is insane,' says Veronica. 'There must be a way through this.'

'There isn't. If you stay here tonight and behave yourselves, I will try to get you out tomorrow on the condition that you turn up at the courthouse on Monday morning. Do you know anyone who would vouch for you and say that you have been upstanding citizens while you have been in Crete?'

'I don't know. We've kept ourselves to ourselves, really.'

'How about `Calista and Cosmos?' says Maria.

'Oh, good shout. Yes - we've seen the two of them every day, and we get on well with them. They run CeeCee Cafe. Their number is in my phone that the police have.'

'Ah, that's great. I know Cosmos well. I will call him. If he comes and vouches for you, I should be able to get you out tomorrow.'

'But we have to stay in jail tonight?'

'Not jail, but here in the police cells. I am sorry, but they require you to because you are foreigners, so you are a flight risk. I'll do everything I can to get you freed in the morning so you can go home and get changed before the court appearance on Monday morning because it will not help your case much if you turn up in court in your nuns' outfits.'

ONCE GUNTHER HAS GONE, we are shown to the police cell, where we must stay the night. To say it's horrible would be unfair to the word 'horrible.' This is nasty on a whole different level. The smell alone makes me want to cry, and it's tiny. I can't see how we're all going to fit in here. I never expected a room with an en suite or anything, but this is ridiculous. And it all feels so unclean, with graffiti on the walls and an overwhelming fear etched into the dismal ceilings and concrete floors.

'Can you imagine the people who have slept in here?' I say. 'If only this cell could talk….'

'If this cell could talk, it would say, 'please clean me and put down some rugs and get some better lights,' says Veronica. 'Honestly, look at the place. It's like we've murdered someone or something. There's no way we can all stay in here. I don't understand why we're being treated like this.'

'We no sleep here,' she says to the officer.

'Yes, sleep. This cell for you to sleep.'

His English isn't as good as the guys we spoke to earlier,

and his manner is atrocious. He points at the beds. 'Enough for sleep,' he says.

He's right: there are eight concrete beds; that's plenty for six of us. But we're practically on top of one another.

'Maybe some more people coming in the night. Now you only six sleep here.'

He bangs the door shut and locks it. Metal on metal. Clanking on clanking. The sound of his heavy footsteps walking away echoing down the narrow corridor.

'Did he say other people might be coming to share the cell with us? Did he?' I say, close to tears.

'Dick-head,' Juan shouts down the corridor.

'It's like they feel personally insulted by how we behaved while wearing the nun's outfits,' says Veronica.

'But they didn't personally see us doing anything. We'd left the club by the time they arrived. We'd have been in cabs on the way home two minutes later, and they'd never have seen us again,' says Juan. 'Why make all this fuss over people going home the next day?'

'I'm not sure 'I'm going home' is much of a defence,' says Veronica. 'I murdered him, but I was about to go home, so leave me alone."

I know she's trying to be the voice of reason and balance, but it's coming over like she thinks they have a valid point.

'You must agree that this is completely over-the-top, Veronica, surely?' I say.

'I do, but I don't know how much value there is in going over how bad it is. Shouldn't we be thinking about what we do now?'

'Yes, we should. But it's also bad.'

'Hang on, what's that?' We hear lots of footsteps coming toward the cell.

'I hope to God it's not criminals come to join us,' I say.

Thankfully, it's not. Instead, it's Gunther and two police officers.

'I'd like five minutes with my clients,' he says.

'We thought you'd gone home,' says Veronica.

'No, I've just been to see whether I can get you out of here tonight, but there's no way. Calista and Cosmos came to the station and gave you glowing references, but they insist that you must stay tonight. They don't want to let you go until after your flight has left tomorrow, in case you try to get onto it.'

'We'll be staying in the hotel, and they know which one it is. So we could promise not to leave the hotel if that would help.'

'No, I'm sorry, but we're out of options. I've spoken to the consulate, and someone will come and meet with you tomorrow. I will come as well. For tonight, though, I'm afraid you have no choice but to stay here.'

'Do they know I'm getting married on Tuesday? I must go home. I can't stay here any longer. This is crazy.'

'It's the way they operate. Maybe next time, choose a different fancy dress theme.'

'Maybe next time we'll choose a different country together.'

With that, he's gone. The sound of the metal door clanging shut reverberates through the concrete cell. The sound of the key turning in the lock and the sound of his boots, heavy on the concrete floors, will stay with me forever.

CHAPTER 18

Leaving the police station the following day is an emotional experience. None of us slept very well, of course. We sat most of the night, trying to think of other people we could invite to the courthouse to vouch for our good character.

'I can't think of anyone,' I say. 'We haven't really talked to people bar Leo at the poolside and the guys at CeeCee's who have already been in to talk to the officers.'

'The manageress of the hotel?'

'I wouldn't have thought so,' I say.

'She might.'

'Let's check with her when we get back. I did annoy her when I wandered down to the kitchen when I was drunk, trying to make cheese on toast.'

'You did what?'

'Yeah – I fell asleep in the lift, and she found me. Didn't I tell you all about this? It was mad. I was drunk and wanted cheese, so I went looking for it. She turned up in my room the next morning because she found my phone in the fridge.'

'My, my, Mary Brown. What other little tricks were you up to when we weren't looking?'

'Just that,' I say. 'That was quite enough.'

Our late-night discussions take in all sorts of subjects, including the wedding and how much we're all looking forward to it. Then to the trickier matter of how we will explain our late arrival home to our partners.

Maria offers to pretend she was ill and that we had to stay to look after her. We debate this route forward as if we are at Prime Ministers' Questions. First, we analyse whether we would all stay if she got ill. I'm sure that, unless it was severe, I would head home to prepare for my nuptials while the others remained with Maria.

'What would prompt all of us not to get our flight back? What could have happened?'

'I guess we could tell the truth,' says Maria. 'We might have to tell the truth if we end up stuck here for another eight weeks.'

'That's not going to happen,' says Juan. 'Come on, let's be positive. It's all going to be OK. We need a little white lie to get us through the next few days.'

'The flight was full?' I venture.

'Is that something they could check, though?' says Charlie.

'Yes, but they wouldn't, would they? It would be really odd if anyone called the airport.'

'But aren't the flights all listed online?'

'I don't know, but I don't think it will say whether they're full. And no one will attempt to book a ticket, just to see whether we're lying, will they?'

'No,' says the others.

So, at 4am, in a cold, smelly police cell, we agree to say that the flight was overbooked, and we were told that we had to fly back on Monday instead of Sunday.

. . .

IT'S incredible how much less threatening the world feels when it's daytime, and you feel the sunlight warming your arm as it streams through the windows and catches your skin. There's a name for that. Juan said it. God, that seems like a long time ago. What was it?

It's 10am, and we're standing at the reception desk, where we've been standing for almost an hour, while officers talk to one another, read through the paperwork, and generally seem unsure what they're doing. Gunther is standing with us and occasionally intervenes, but it's all in Greek, so no one knows what's happening.

'Apricity!' I say, rather too loudly. 'I was trying to remember the word you taught us, Juan. It's apricity, isn't it?'

'It is,' says Juan, with a smile. 'You've learned a lot on this trip, haven't you?'

'Oh yes,' I say. 'I've learned a new word for targeted sunlight and never to dress as a nun.'

'OK, you are free to go,' says Gunther, shuffling papers around. 'This is the information relating to the charges against you. There's quite a lot for us to discuss. Shall I keep hold of this? And I will call you in a couple of hours when I have managed to talk to someone at the consulate, and we will meet this afternoon to discuss it all and prepare you for the court appearance in the morning.'

'Yes, that sounds like a good idea,' I say. 'Can I take your number?'

He hands over his rather flashy-looking card and double-checks that he has my number, then we're off.

'Come on, let's head for the border?' says Charlie, running down the steps.

'Well, we could, but this is an island. Our only chance of escape is to swim for the mainland. So I think we might be better served by just turning up tomorrow and getting on with it,' advises Juan.

WE GET a cab back to the hotel, all feeling drained and too introspective to celebrate the fact that we are free. We all recognise that while we are free for now, this time tomorrow, if someone turns up at the courthouse and says that we offended them, we might be in a whole heap of trouble.

We pull up outside Hotel Xenia and decide to go in, shower, and meet back downstairs in half an hour to go for breakfast at CeeCee's. We want to thank Cosmos and Calista for coming to the station to give us a positive reference, and we're all starving and in desperate need of coffee.

As the others climb out of the cab, I grab Juan's arm and pull him back into his seat beside me.

'I'm worried,' I say, unable to keep my thoughts inside my head any longer. 'I'm worried that I won't be there for my wedding, and I'm worried that if Ted finds out what happened, he won't want to marry me.'

'Don't be so ridiculous,' says Juan. 'That's crazy. First, he won't find out; if he did, he'd think it was funny.'

'No, he wouldn't. I know Ted. He'd be appalled that I was flashing. He was even fussing about which underwear I could take with me. He'd be cross if he heard that I flashed my bottom at a big party. Particularly if it led to us having to postpone the wedding.'

'Look - that's not going to happen. Look at me.'

I lift my head from its position, looking down into my lap, and look into his eyes. He can see they are full of tears.

'Come here,' he says, wrapping me in a huge hug. 'We're a big group of people from a powerful country. We're not going to end up in jail; we're not going to have any problems beyond today. This will be something we laugh about in a few years. We'll shake our heads whenever we catch up and remember our dramatic holiday in Crete. It'll be our secret.'

'He can't find out. He really can't.'

'He won't,' says Veronica, leaning into the cab to see what's going on. 'We all promised each other last night that no one would say anything to anyone about this, and none of us will. So there won't be a problem. We'll fly home tomorrow, and we will all be there to see you get married to the man of your dreams on Tuesday.'

'Yes, but...'

'No buts. The guys will think we had an extra day on the weekend because of flight problems. They'll never be any the wiser. We know it will go well in the courthouse tomorrow. No one's going to come and complain. Come on. We're here. Let's all go and get a shower and some breakfast; then everything will feel better.'

There are lots of hugs for me as we get out of the car and lots of repetitions of what Veronica has just told me; it's all going to be okay, and Ted will never know about our ludicrous behaviour.

We thank the driver and walk towards the colossal hotel door. I'm still worried. My stomach's churning, but I appreciate everything my friends say. I'll feel better when I've had reassurances from the man at the consulate.

As we approach the door to the hotel, it is pulled open by Agata.

'Hello, thank you very much,' says Juan, moving past her.

'Here are your things in your bags,' she says with an angry look.

All our bags sit just inside the doorway, in the dark hallway. They are like a group of children waiting at an after-school club to be collected by their parents.

'We were hoping we'd be able to stay an extra night,' Juan says. 'We missed our flight this morning.'

'You go now,' she says. 'No stay here.'

'Are the rooms all booked tonight?' I ask. It seems odd that they would be empty all weekend and then booked on a Sunday night.

'No rooms are booked,' she says. 'All rooms are free, but you no stay here.'

'Why?'

'You insult religion. You anger everyone. You must go.'

'Come on,' says Karren. She scratches her head as she speaks, making her hair stand out like a halo around her head. Sleeping overnight in a police cell without access to basic toiletries and electrical appliances has left us all looking homeless. 'You must let us stay tonight. We've got nowhere else to go, and all our things are here. We'll leave in the morning.'

'No,' she says simply. 'I cannot have you here. Not after what you have done.'

'But what have we done? We were just having fun.'

'You have disgraced yourselves. You will not disgrace my name. Now go.'

'Please. You must see how unfair this is,' I say. 'If we're found to have done something wrong, we'll be dealt with by the courts tomorrow. If not, we're innocent. It's not up to you to decide.'

'Leave now,' says Agata. 'Go, or I call the police and tell them you are being a nuisance.'

'Let's get out of here,' says Karren. 'This will make things much worse if we're not careful.'

We pick up our bags and walk back onto the road. Agata walks into the hotel, closing the heavy oak door behind her. There's a thump as it shuts and the sound of her turning the key in the lock.

'Fuck you,' shouts Veronica. 'Fuck you all.'

. . .

It's 3pm when we meet Gunther and a man called Emmett from the British consulate in Crete. Emmett is more casual than Gunther, opting for a cardigan with his shirt and tie. When he removes the navy knitwear, I see a short-sleeved shirt underneath. Gunther makes no such concessions to the weather. He's in a dark grey suit, white shirt, and blue tie. I have no idea about the sleeve length he's gone for today because he doesn't remove his jacket. Honestly, it's about a million degrees in the shade, and the man is dressed for winter in London. Emmett has brought a man called Oliver with him, but Oliver doesn't engage a great deal; he just takes notes while Emmett speaks.

We're in a backroom at CeeCee's because we had nowhere else to go. We have found a hotel that suits us just fine, but it's not great for business meetings. It has no quiet area in which we would be able to talk to our legal team, and I didn't fancy inviting them to a meeting in one of our bedrooms. Being the Sabbath and all that, we may find out that it's a crime and end up in prison for the rest of our lives.

'This is not an uncommon situation,' says Emmett, in a calm, reassuring manner. 'There have been lots of stag weekends that have ended up offending local tastes and found themselves in court, only for no one to turn up and complain, allowing them to leave the country.'

'Oh great. So that always happens, does it?'

'In my experience, certainly. In the cases we have researched this morning, there has been no follow-on action after the court appearance.'

'Oh wow, that's such a relief,' I say. 'Oh my God, I can hardly breathe; I've been so worried; I'm due to get married on Tuesday, and if they….'

'OK, let me just stop you there. I was going to go on to say that there haven't been any follow-on problems relating to the religious offence charges. But in this case, there are other issues. The police gave your lawyer some notes he passed on to me today, highlighting other concerns they have been alerted to concerning your behaviour while in Crete. I think it would be useful to run through some of the issues that have arisen, and perhaps you could offer your thoughts on them?'

'Yes, very happy to,' I say.

'They all relate to your time on the island.'

'OK. We've done nothing wrong since we came here. Only the incident in the hotel with the flashing. That's all.'

'Sure, well, we might be able to deal with these issues quite easily then. I'll go through them one by one, and if you could provide a response between you, that would be very useful.'

'Sure,' I say, and he pulls a stack of papers out of his bag.

'Gosh, that's a lot of sheets of paper. How many misdemeanours do they think we have committed?' I ask.

'Quite a few,' says Gunther. 'Quite a few.'

CHAPTER 19

'Let's go through all the issues the police have raised as 'being of concern' and 'likely to cause offence,' and they plan to raise in court tomorrow. You should be aware that if these need further investigation, we will have to postpone the court date for a few weeks while we gather your defence.'

'I can't,' I say. 'My wedding is on Tuesday. So I must go back tomorrow.'

'I'm afraid it's not going to be that simple. Trust me: it's in your interests that we clear this up and mount a proper defence. So let's go through these.'

Christ. What on earth am I going to do?

'The first point they raise is that when you arrived on Thursday, you drove past a police officer and deliberately caused such a commotion that she could not do her work.'

'That wasn't us!' we all shriek.

'That was the cab driver,' Veronica clarifies. 'We had nothing to do with it. We didn't know he would turn the music high to annoy her. How can we possibly be to blame for his actions? Anyway, I got the impression that he knew the officer and was fooling around with her.'

'Do you know the taxi driver's name?'

'No. He was just having fun. This is crazy. How can this possibly be our responsibility?'

Oliver scribbles in his notebook while we talk. Gunther says something in Greek. Emmett nods and scribbles on his notes.

'There's also an issue concerning Mary stealing food from the hotel kitchen.'

'What?'

'The hotel manager says that you went down into the kitchens on Friday evening and helped yourself to food.'

'I had a piece of toast,' I said. 'Really? We'll go to court over having a piece of toast from the hotel kitchen.'

'You weren't authorised to take it.'

'She showed me where the kitchen was after she found me asleep in the lift. Oh, for heaven's sake, this is crazy. I'm on my hen weekend, and I fancied a piece of toast.'

'OK, I don't think that will cause too much of a problem. The next point is that Juan attempted to board a yacht and claimed he was looking for George Clooney.'

'Yes. I was looking for George Clooney. I thought it would be fun for Mary to meet him since she's on her hen weekend.'

'Were you drunk?'

'No.'

'So, why did you board the boat.'

'I was looking for George Clooney.'

'We need you to be completely honest and straightforward with us. The Police will be keen to establish the real reason for your visit to the boat. Especially since they were watching the boat then, and they later arrested the crew on drug smuggling charges.'

'I went there to try and see George Clooney. That's the truth. He's in Crete. I was told he was on the boat. Veronica, show them the pictures.'

Veronica pulls out her phone and shows the men the pictures she has.

'We went off on land, looking for him, and Juan swam out to sea. It was all so innocent and done to give Mary some pictures.'

'I didn't know who or what was on the boat, but the guy at the café thought Clooney was on board,' says Juan.

Hearing our explanations, and seeing the pictures, seems to have reassured them a little.

'We'll run that all passed them,' says Emmett. Then he turns to Gunther. 'The police must know that Clooney is here. So why are they concerned about Juan's explanation?'

Gunther shakes his head and raises his shoulders.

'Let's continue through this list. I have a note that you used the facilities in Hotel Cristina without permission.'

'That's untrue. We sat by the pool and had drinks, which we paid for. We never used the pool's facilities. As soon as the staff told us to move, we did. And we were with Leo that day, Gunther's friend. He explained to the staff at the hotel that we were his guests. You can check with him.'

Oliver continues to scribble in his notebook. The two men look at one another.

'There's another note about that day. It says you were wearing an offensive t-shirt, Juan, and you flirted in a homosexual way with a barman working at the public bar.'

'I certainly did not,' says Juan. 'I am very sorry if the t-shirt caused offence, but the word on it was in English, and since we are in Crete, I had ever reason to think that people wouldn't be able to read it.'

'And you would deny that you flirted with the barman.'

'Absolutely,' he says.

The frustrating thing about all these accusations is that they are, strictly speaking, true, but they are so petty. Would you really expect to get hauled up in front of the police for wearing a t-shirt with 'bitch' on it? No. A gentle warning is the most you would expect. But I worry that when they're put with the principal charge that we were being rude to their religion, it makes us look like thugs who should be locked away.

'Is there anything else?'

'There are issues like excessive drinking and the fact that when the hotel manageress knocked on your bedroom door, Mary, you were in bed with a man, and you are getting married soon. The hotel owner said that she found that offensive.'

'Ooooo Mary, who were you in bed with?' asks Charlie.

'With Juan. We both woke up early, then decided to go back to bed. It was no big deal, And does she have any right to complain about what I do in my room? I wasn't breaking the law.'

'No, none of these things are highlighted because the police suggest that you were breaking the law. The worry is that they feed into the character judgements that will be made of you and may make the primary accusation stick.'

'I think it's ridiculous. We didn't offend anyone. We spent most of our time at CeeCee's cafe, and they seem to like us there. We are pretty sure that we know who called the police on us, someone who didn't like us talking to her boyfriend at the hotel. This is all a complete stitch up,' I say.

'OK, there's no need for raised voices,' says Emmett.

'But there is a need for raised voices. This is all ludicrous.'

'I understand your frustration, but you must be calm and respectful tomorrow. You will need to apologise for any offence caused and not raise your voice or become angry.'

'I won't,' I say.

'Gunther will stay with you now and run through what will happen in the morning. You need to come to the courthouse, smartly dressed, at 9am. I will prepare a response to the complaints we've discussed today. Is there anything else you wish to say?'

Emmett and his scribbling protege leave, and we all sit in silence, shaking our heads.

'If you think of anything else that has happened since you've been here, let me know so I'm not confronted by any surprises in the morning,' says Gunther.

'We will,' we say. I'm tempted to lash back with, 'I think I forgot to brush my teeth properly one morning,' but I decide not to. I can see that Emmett is right. I will try to control my runaway mouth. The way forward is to nod sweetly and smile elegantly.

'Right, let me talk through the morning and what you can expect to see. Dies anyone want another coffee?'

'Can I have a fishbowl of mojito?' I say, with a hopeful smile.

'I don't know what that is, and I sense that you are joking, but if it's alcoholic, the answer is 'no.' I think it would be very wise not to drink any alcohol today. Stay low-key. Base yourselves in the hotel and keep yourselves to yourselves. Understood?'

'Understood,' we chorus back.

'So, coffees?'

CHAPTER 20

They design these buildings to terrify people. They must do. The massive door, the imposing structure of the room, with the judges sitting high and mighty, and us sitting lower down, looking up at them, begging for mercy. The place has a gladiatorial feel. If the plan of the architects of Crete's courthouse was to drive fear into the hearts of anyone forced to appear here, their plan worked a treat. I am well and truly terrified.

I'll admit that when we arrived here this morning, I was feeling confident, even a little angry that we were being put through this madness. Speaking to mum and Ted didn't help, of course, They were both alarmed when I called them yesterday and told them that the flight was full. 'But you have exceptional circumstances for getting on the flight. Tell the people you booked the flight with, ring the company in charge. 'Is there anything I can do to help?' asked Ted. At one point mum even suggested that I should call the British Embassy in Crete to complain. How ironic. I didn't tell mum that I was on first name terms with the bloke from the Embassy!

I tried to explain that airlines are legitimately allowed to overbooked flights, and we've been unlucky to be the ones thrown off. 'I guess it's because we're a big group.'

'No, I'm sure this isn't right,' mum kept saying. I really thought she was going to start ringing the airline company herself. In desperation I made the mistake of saying that I would call the airlines first thing in the morning to complain and see whether they could get me on an early flight. That meant me having to phone her again this morning from the car, on the way to the courthouse to tell her that there were no flights until this afternoon.

'They're lying to you. There are lots of flights this morning,' mum said.

'I know, but they're all full.'

'Really? Every single one.'

'Yep. I guess it's the time of year.'

'Oh darling, this is awful. What are we going to do?'

Next I had to call Ted.

'Sweetheart, we're getting married tomorrow. You have to get on a flight today. What are they playing at. I'm going to see what Mike can do. He might have police contacts in Crete. 'No!' I squealed, rather too loudly. 'No, darling, I'm handling it. They're looking at flights. Let's not get too heavy-handed with things. Let me deal with this and I'll see you later.'

The hens are all looking at me as I make my calls. When I hand up and give a huge sigh, they sigh too. 'We'll get you home for that wedding. Somehow, whatever we must do, we'll get you home,' says Juan. He's no more able to get me home than he can fight a lion or with gold in the Olympic women's gymnastics, but I do appreciate the sentiments and the vast kindness and support behind the words.

Now we're all sitting in the courthouse waiting for the judge to arrive. We're dressed to be as inoffensive as possible, the exact opposite of how Juan usually dresses but bless him, he's done his best. He looks very demure, particularly wearing the tie Oliver was instructed to remove from his own neck and hand to Juan.

'Look,' says Maria. 'Isn't that Lina?'

We look to the other side of the court room where a tall, elegant lady in a black shift dress walks through. She waves to a man, standing by the public gallery, and walks over to him.

'That looks like scar man,' says Juan. 'That's the police officer who was in the station, and I'm pretty sure he's the guy who was with Lina on the pool deck. I have a horrible feeling that we're about to get stitched up.'

'No, this is not happening,' says Juan. 'Does anyone have a pen and paper?'

Between us we produce a pen and a scrap of paper which Juan hands to Karren. 'My handwriting is terrible, as is my spelling. Could you write this down for me?' he says.

'Dear Lina, My name is Juan. I and my friends have been in Crete celebrating the fact that my friend is getting married tomorrow. We have no idea why you are trying to cause trouble for you, but I PROMISE YOU – we will cause far more trouble for you if you don't leave the courthouse. We saw you with your lover on the pool deck, the guy you're standing next to now. We have photos. We will send those photos to Leo.'

The issue now was to get the note to Lina on the other side of the room. We couldn't really leave the area we'd been told to stand in, and we couldn't throw it across the room. 'Oh hell, just give it to me, I'll run over there,' says Maria. 'I once saved the life of a fish. I can do anything.'

We watch as she makes the dash across the room, and drops the note in Lina's hand, then bolts back. She's beside us, slightly out of breath, but beaming with delight, before anyone notices she's been missing.

We all look over at Lina who looks at us then turns her back to read the letter. She clearly thought we wouldn't recognise her.

While Lina reads, Emmett comes over and tells us that there's a bit of a problem. Someone has turned up at the courthouse to complain. It means the charge against us will stick, and we will have to face the judge today. He is worried about preparing a proper defence. He will talk to the judge now. Across the other side of the courtroom there's no sign of Lina.

'Do you think he's talking about someone else complaining, or do you think it's just Lina?' I say.

'He said 'someone' so hopefully it's just her. I thought she might send a note back though. I'm confused about what's happening now.'

'Hi,' says Gunther, coming over to join us. 'Feeling OK?'

'Nervous,' I say. 'And a bit confused about what's going on. Has someone come to the courthouse to complain about us?'

'I'm afraid they have.'

'Just one person?'

'Yes, just one. As we predicted, it's the same person who called the Police on Saturday night. Emmett has gone to talk to her.'

'So, it's a woman?'

'It is, yes,' he says. 'Let me go and check on Emmett. I'll be back in five minutes.'

Once Gunther is out of earshot, Juan turns to me. 'How bloody weird is all this. If Gunther is a friend of Leo's, he must realise that it's Leo's girlfriend who's doing the complaining.'

'Yeah, I guess. Though I don't know whether they're friends, or just business associates.'

There's a commotion at the front of the courtroom where

the grand seats reside, and a court official motions for us to stand. We clamber to our feet, and three men walk in and take their seats. Gunther and Emmett rush back to our sides.

'It's all fine,' whispers Gunther, just stay standing and address the judge.'

The judge talks in Greek, then turns to address us.

'You are brought here today because you are judged to have caused a scandal by provocative acts and by misrepresenting a uniform. I will now ask those present whether there is anyone who agrees that you have caused a scandal.'

She speaks in Greek again, and we all hold hands. I also hold my breath. I'm terrified to breathe incase it's misinterpreted as a call out from the small crows that has gathered.

There's silence.

She seems to wait for ages before speaking in Greek again.

Then she turns to us and tells us that we are free to go.

'We can go? Leave?' I say to Gunther.

'Yes, the woman who came in earlier has left. So you are free to go.'

I scream, then stop myself. I turn back to the judge and thank her profusely. She smiles and nods, and we keep thanking her. We thank Gunther, Emmett, and poor Oliver, who's been sitting there without a tie.

'You are all amazing I'll never forget what you have done for us. Thank you, from the bottom of my heart.'

'You may go now,' repeats the judge. She stands up and leaves the room.

That's when the celebrations really start, we hug and kiss one another and dance around like we've just won the World Cup.

'Right, to the airport then,' I say. 'Let's get home and get all dressed up. I'm getting married in the morning.'

. . .

We stand a few metres from the check-in desk at the airport, wondering what to do next. It doesn't feel like a few days since we arrived at this airport for our fabulous weekend of food, drink, and merriment. It feels like a lifetime ago. If I'd known what would happen, I'd have stayed on the plane and gone back home again.

'What the hell are we going to do? How are we going to get back?' I ask the others. Shall I go up to the desk and explain what's happened.

'No, you stay there. Leave it to me,' says Juan, walking towards the counter with a gentle swagger of his shoulders and a shimmy in his hips. I've no idea what he's going to try, but I hope it works. I need to get home pronto; I should be at home, helping mum to decorate the pretty gardening school that needs to pass for a wedding venue, not standing around in a crowded airport.

We walk Juan walk towards the airline officials, stop, turn on his heels, and come cat-walking back to us.

'None of those guys is gay' he says with a grimace. 'So annoying.' It's as if he thinks the airport officials are being deliberately obtuse. 'Come with me Veronica.'

Good decision, I think to myself. If you're going to try to get men to help you, you need Veronica in your camp.

The two of them are gone for ages, giving me time to call mum and tell her that we're at the airport and I expect to be on a flight soon.

'We're at the gardening school, sorting things out. It's looking lovely, Mary, you'll be really pleased,' she says.

'Oh, thank you so much, mum. I can't wait to see you.'

'And we can't wait to see you, love. Ted is so worried. Do you want me to call him and reassure him.'

'Oh, yes please, mum. Tell him I'll let him know the flight details as soon as they're confirmed. I should know very soon.'

I hang up and look down at my phone. I want to send a message to Leo to thank him for his help and to let him know that everything is fine and I'm on my way home, but I also want to tell him about Lina. Should I do that? I want him to know what a snake she is, but then I'm also very grateful that she left the courthouse when she did. I really don't want any more trouble from that woman.'

'Hey Leo, Thanks for all your help. You were a complete star, and Gunther was wonderful. All was fine this morning, so we're at the airport waiting to go home.'

I put the phone away and see Juan and Veronica walking towards us with two airport officials.

'Here we go, we're going to be on the next flight out of here.' I say to Karren.

Juan eases himself to the head of the other three and walks towards me. He has a very serious look on his face as if there is something he must convey to me urgently.

'Hold your head and pretend it hurts,' he says.

'What?'

'Come on, just do it,' his words are thrown at me with a considerable amount of aggression. Without waiting a moment longer, I drop my head into my hands, and stand there holding it for no reason.

'What's the matter?' asks Karren, putting her arm around my shoulders.'

'No questions, no comments,' spits Juan, just as the two officials catch up with him.

'You must be Mary. How are you feeling?' asks one of the men, reaching out to touch my shoulder.

'She's really not very well,' Juan says. 'It was a nasty car crash, and she was thrown into the side of the car.'

'Car crash?' I say.

'Yes,' says one of the men, kindly. He's small and tubby. His colleague is long and lean. They couldn't look more ridiculous together. I'm sure that whoever does the airport staff rota deliberately put them together for fun. 'Don't you remember the crash?' he asks.

'Oh, it's awful,' says Juan. 'Her memory has gone. She remembers nothing since it happened. It's all quite shocking.'

'Have you been to the hospital? It sounds like a brain injury. I think she should be seen urgently by an expert in these things. I'm not sure she's OK to fly?'

'Yes, perfect to fly,' says Juan. 'She told me that she might feel a little brighter if she could get up into the air. The sooner we can get her on a flight, the better.'

By now, I realise precisely what Juan is doing: the car crash is to explain why we missed our flights, and the drama about my injuries is to convince British Airways that I need to head home urgently.

'I would be more comfortable booking her onto a flight if she'd had medical clearance to fly,' says the short, round man.

'Please fly me,' I say in a weird, contorted voice that makes everyone stop and stare at me.

'I need to get home. I'll feel much better if I can see my doctor at home.'

'That's right. We are planning to take her straight to the hospital back in England. That's what she really wants to do.'

'Come and sit down over here.' It's the very tall slim man who is talking now. He has a warm, friendly face that one doesn't usually associate with the painfully thin. Added to that, his trousers are not quite long enough, and they flap around the top of his socks, so he looks like a schoolboy who's grown out of his clothes at the end of term. Or an airport executive who is so tall that none of the regulation trousers fit him properly. I am dying to tell him that he ought to complain about them; he's entitled to have trousers that fit if he's being made to wear a uniform. I can't tell him this, of course, because I have amnesia brought on by a car crash that forced me to miss my flight this morning.

I sit down and drop my head into my hands.

'We'll see what we can do,' says the tall man with the short trousers. '

The flights are jam-packed, though,' says the short man. 'If we can get you onto one, we will, but we'll need to get you seen by a doctor first.'

'And you have no other injuries? You're not bleeding anywhere?' asks tall man.

'No.'

'OK, let's see whether we can get the two of you onto the next flight, and the rest of your party onto the flight after that. How does that sound?'

'That would be great,' I say. 'I'd really be grateful if you could get me home.'

I MANAGE NOT to have to see a doctor. I'm not sure how. The guys seemed determined that I couldn't fly before I was examined, but I kept saying, 'It's such a short flight, I'm sure I'll be fine,' and they suddenly agreed. I'm now at the departure gate with Juan. I'm so relieved. I thought I was going to miss my wedding. Juan wraps his arm around me, and we sit there waiting to be called onto the plane.

CHAPTER 21

The arrival at Heathrow is a mixed blessing. I'm pleased to be back after the dramas that unfolded in Crete. The dramas that we will NEVER SPEAK OF. There have been times over the past few days when England felt so far away. I thought I'd never be back. But now I'm sitting here, waiting to disembark, part of me wishes I was still in Crete because I am dreading all the lies I am going to have to tell to everyone today and tomorrow, and at the wedding. I'm dreading having to moan about the airline, and everyone saying how unfortunate we were. I hate lying and I'm going to have to do a whole load of it for the next few days.

Ted has said he'll meet me at the airport, so the first lie will be to him. I stand up and move to get my bag from the locker.

'No, please, Madam, don't worry about that. We'll get your bag for you.'

'Oh, thank you,' I say. 'There's a pink bag and a brown envelope that I need to try and keep flat.'

'No problem,' she says.

'What envelop?' asks Juan.

'It's the picture. Do you remember? That artist drew a picture of me when we went to the market.'

'Oh yes, oh – I'm so glad you've still got that. Make sure you get it framed.'

'OK, we're ready for you now, Madam,' says the air hostess. She has my bags and his holding her hand out to assist me.

The rest of the passengers are held back while Juan and I are taken off the plane. When exit into the airport there's a doctor waiting with a man pushing a wheelchair.

'Oh God,' I say to Juan. 'Do I really have to sit in that?'

'Just do it,' he says. 'Do whatever they say, and let's get out of here quickly.'

I am pushed through the building, which is quite pleasant, then asked dozens of questions by the doctor. He takes my temperature, my blood pressure and he checks in my eyes. Then he moves my head around in circles.

'Everything seems to be OK,' he says. 'Where is the pain?'

'The pain's gone,' I say. 'I took a painkiller, and it seems much better now. Thank you so much for all your help.'

'Not a problem. You'll still need to keep an eye on it, though. How are you getting home?' he asks.

'My fiancé is meeting me,' I say. 'He'll be just through the other side, by customs. Juan can push me.'

'No, not a problem. Marcus will come with you, just to make sure you're still feeling OK. Make sure you drink lots of water, take painkillers if you need to, and if you have any light-headedness, tingling, or feel faint or excessively tired, you must go straight to A&E and get properly checked out. OK?'

'OK,' I say, and Marcus pushes me through customs, while Juan carries all my things. I keep glancing at him, but don't catch his eye. I'm not quite sure how we're going to explain this to Ted. It adds more complexity to an already pretty damn complex story.

We couldn't get on the flight because it was full, so they made us wait until the next day then insisted I sit in a wheelchair. How does that make any sense?

I see Ted straight away, standing near the back of the line, looking hopefully as people stream past. When he sees the wheelchair his face falls and he rushes over.

'Who is that with him?' asks Juan.

'Oh God, that's Mike. Oh no. Why the hell is Mike here?'

'Hi gorgeous,' says Ted, bending down to kiss me. 'What the hell happened.'

'We'll tell you in a minute,' says Juan. 'Marcus, we'll be absolutely fine now. Thanks for your help.'

'Are you sure? I can go all the way to the carpark if you'd like.'

'No need at all. I'm fine. Honestly. Thank you very much.'

Ted takes the bags, handing a couple to Mike, I stand up out of the wheelchair, and Marcus heads off.

'So why the wheelchair? Have you hurt yourself?'

I don't know what to say. I'm all out of lies.

'The flights were very full again today so we said that Mary wasn't very well in order to guarantee her a seat. The others are having to come back on a later flight.'

'Oh,' says Mike. 'That seems strange. Why is every flight out of Crete suddenly full to the brim? It's not normally like that.'

'No idea,' I say.

'So when will the rest of the girls be coming back? They'll be there for the wedding, won't they?'

'Oh yes, they should get a flight back tonight.'

'Unless they're all full,' says Mike. 'Because, as we know, everyone is leaving Crete at the moment.'

Honestly, he's such a tosser.

'It's lovely to see you, Mike, but why did you come to the airport? I'm sure you must have better things to do with your time?'

'Ted's staying at mine tonight, remember, so the bride can get ready in peace tomorrow. He didn't have his car with him, so I drove.'

'That's very kind of you.'

We get to Mike's car and he starts loading the bags into the boot.

He holds the brown envelope in his hands.

'Can I ned this?' he asks.

'No! It's a picture of me. Painted by a street artist in Crete.'

'Oh let me see,' says Ted, pulling open the envelope and retrieving the picture. Mike looks over his shoulder.

'What are you wearing?' he asks.

'Oh, I was dressed as a nun.'

'You were dressed as a nun in Crete. A nun with makeup on?'

'Yes,' I say. 'The theme was the Sound of Music.'

'And you all went out dressed as nuns and got drunk and partied?'

'Is there a problem with that?'

'Not at all.'

Like I keep saying – tosser.

CHAPTER 22

'I'm getting married!' I shriek. 'Me, married.'

'I know, love. I know,' says Juan, offering me a pained smile.

'No need to look so glum. It's a good thing,' I remind him. 'Just 24 hours ago we didn't know whether we'd ever be coming back to England, let alone back in time for the wedding. Now here we are…on my special day.'

'I know love, it's wonderful. We're going to make this the best day ever. I'm really pleased for you.'

'Then tell your face because your face doesn't look at all pleased; it looks like a smacked arse.'

'Sorry,' says Juan, laughing at my comment. 'I just feel so guilty about everything.'

'What do you mean, you feel guilty?'

'I caused all the problems. It was me who put you through all that misery and pain by making you wear a nun's habit and prance around like an idiot. I should have thought about things more carefully and worked out where we were. I'm sorry.'

'Hey, stop it. You were amazing. You got me on the flight

home, you looked after me, and now – here we are – about to have the best wedding day in the history of the world.'

'Yeah, but I got you home by telling them that you had a car crash, thus causing even more problems.'

'It was fine. I even got to ride in a wheelchair through the terminal.'

'Yes, but what a chaotic way to get home. And the day before you get married. Everything I do ends in disaster.'

'Hey, love, you're preaching to the choir here. I've never done anything that hasn't ended up in total and unadulterated mayhem and madness. It doesn't matter. We're fit, healthy and alive. The rest of the group is coming back this morning. We'll all be there for the wedding. It's all good.'

'But it was bloody terrifying. It's all my fault. I'm sorry.'

'Stop saying sorry or I'm going to drop you from the bridesmaid team. You'll be on the bench or bringing on the oranges half-way down the aisle or something.'

'OK, no more apologising.'

'Good.'

Juan is in bed with me. I know this isn't how most brides-to-be wake up on their wedding morning, but we ended up talking half the night, and I wanted him to stay near me. Because, as much as I'm reassuring Juan endlessly about my state of mind, and that none of it matters, I do feel quite shaken everything that happened. I can still hear those prison doors slam shut, and the sound of the key in the lock. If I think about it too much, I feel my stomach turn.

'We should probably get up,' I say. 'There's so much to do. I need to ring mum. I'm dreading it. I've lied to her so much.'

'Yes, to protect her.'

'I know but I never lie to mum. I hate lying to her. Who lies to their mum, for God's sake?'

'A woman who has no choice if she wants to protect her mum and prevent her mum from worrying, that's who.'

'Thanks,' I say. 'I need to pick up my dress soon, and if it doesn't fit, I'm buggered.'

'OK. Ring your mum now, talk to her, I'll track down the guys in Crete and see whether they know what flight they're on, then we'll do a list of everything that has to be organised and I'll get onto it.'

I pick up the phone and tentatively call my mum. She sounds so relieved to hear my voice that I feel guilty all over again.

'Oh thank goodness,' she says. 'Oh, I've been so worried. Even though you texted to say you were back last night, it's lovely to hear your voice.'

'It's lovely to hear yours too, mum,' I say, choking back tears. 'Everything's OK. Today's my wedding day. Hoorah! We're going to have a lovely time. Juan is with me and he's keen to help in any way we need it.'

'Oh good. I'm glad Juan is with you. Next time, just go out for a night in London. That's what Ted and his friends did for the stag night. They had a lovely time.'

'Yes, you're right mum. If I decide to get married again, that's exactly what I'll do, but shall we get this wedding done first, before planning the next one.'

There's a silence on the end of the phone as she works out whether to berate me further.

'I could really do with your help, mum,' I say.

'Of course.'

I list the things I'm worried about, prompted by Juan and his notebook.

'I need to collect the dress from the alteration people and try it on, and I need to collect the bridesmaids' dresses. I need to pick up flowers and take them to the venue, I need to make sure the car is coming, and I must get my nails done and get myself ready. Shit, there's a lot to do. And I must pick up my shoes as well.

Oh, and I need to double-check the photographer is all OK.'

'Well, no need to worry because I've done most of that. I have the dress here, ready for you to try on. I think it'll be fine unless you've put on loads of weight on the hen weekend. I've also got your shoes and the bridesmaids dresses.'

'Oh wow, mum - thank you so much. That's such a relief.'

I mouth to Juan that mum has sorted things out.

'I love you,' I say. 'I'm really sorry I worried you.'

I can feel tears welling in the backs of my eyes again. I am sorry that I worried mum so much, and I feel awful that I can't tell her the truth. I'll let her know the truth one day, but today is not that day.

'Don't worry. It's all OK now,' she says. 'As long as you're safely back, that's all that matters.'

'Your father and I will be over to yours later this morning. Let's say 11am, shall we? Will the bridesmaids be there?'

'Yes, they'll all be here,' I say, looking at Juan. He just shrugs at me. He's obviously no wiser than I am.

Where the hell are my bridesmaids?

I leave Juan on bridesmaid duty, as continues to call them, and checks the flights out of Crete that morning, trying to work out which ones they might have to have caught.

'The fact that none of them are answering phones may indicate that they're in the air right now,' he says.

'Or they have been re-arrested after someone turned up at the courthouse to complain about us.'

'Let's go with 'they're on the plane' shall we?'

The main tasks of the day all involve making me look like a bride.

First, it's the task of trying on my wedding dress and shoes. By some wonderous luck, it all fits perfectly. My spirits are lifted as soon as I realise I'm going to be OK. The dress looks good. I won't have to wear a habit instead (too soon for nun jokes?) Next, it's my nails. I know the photographer will want to get shots of the rings, so my nails need to look good. I go for a pearly white, virginal, wedding-appropriate look.

Then, Jackie, the hairdresser, arrives. She's an interesting choice as a hairdresser because her own locks are in a dreadful state. She has one side shaved with a tattoo on her skull, and the other side hangs to her chin, pink and limp. You feel that if she is as good at hairdressing as we all hope she is, she'd do something a little more flattering with her own hair.

But, she has a good reputation, so I try to relax while she works her magic, washing, brushing, teasing, combing, rolling and spraying my locks into place.

She's not doing my hair Infront of a mirror, because we're in my sitting room, so it's not until the end that I get to see what she's done.

I walk into the bedroom, with Jackie close behind, clutching her comb.

I look into the mirror with some concern. What if it's awful? I wasn't here for the practice appointment yesterday, so neither of us knows how this is going to go.

'Oh wow.'

It looks wonderful. It's kind of half up, half down, with lovely flowers dotted through it, and tendrils of hair gently caressing my shoulders. I've never looked so good.

'I want you to come and live with me, and do my hair every day,' I say.

'Ha. Ha. You'd soon get fed up with me. I'm glad you like it though. You look fab. Have a wonderful day.'

The next to work her magic is Janine, the make-up artist who begins by cleansing my face. While she wipes her magic lotions over me, I notice Jackie tutting every time Janine goes near my hair. Jackie responds by sighing deeply. I glance at Juan, and he stifles a laugh. I hope these two aren't going to start fighting, that really would be the perfect end to my unconventional wedding preparations. Steve and David, the photographers arrive next and begin snapping us as we get ready. I try to look elegant and sophisticated, but with Juan making faces at me, the hairdresser and the make-up artist almost coming to blows over the state of my tendrils, and dad sitting in the corner minding his own business, the bizarre humour gets to me, and I find myself laughing instead of pouting.

Janine adds a second layer of contouring to my jawline (I know, I know, it's ridiculous, but it's my wedding day, so give me a break, OK), while Juan makes valiant attempts to reach the hens. My phone rings. It's an unknown number.

'Oh wow, this could be the hens in Crete.'

I answer the phone, despite objections from Janine who wants to add translucent powder under my cheekbones.

'Hello, Mary Brown speaking.'

'Oh hello, my name is Melodie Breakspeare. I'm a journalist from the Daily Mail doing the story about your arrest in Crete. Can I check a few details with you?'

'I'm sorry, not right now I'm just preparing to get married.'

'Bloody PPI,' I say to mum and dad.

'Great. Let's just add moon dust to your temples,' Janine says. 'Then we can sort out your eyelashes.'

While she speaks, I am glaring at Juan, trying to communicate the details of the call I just had, without using words.

'Oh, it's my phone now,' says mum, wandering off into the other room to take the call. 'I bet this will be Aunty Susan. Did I tell you she's gone to the palace this morning, just to make sure everything looks OK.'

'That's really kind of her,' I reply.

Once mum's out of earshot, chatting to Aunty Susan in the kitchen, I swing round to face Juan.

'That was the bloody Daily Mail,' I say. 'They are running a story about us being arrested and wanted to check all the facts.'

'What? How did they find out?'

'I don't know. Perhaps it was in the news in Crete? What are we going to do?'

'Nothing,' he says. 'We're going to ignore it all and concentrate on the wedding. Nothing else matters.'

'But what if they write about it?'

'There's nothing we can do to stop that, just don't talk to them and try and forget about it.'

'OK.'

Mum returns to the room with a big smile on her face. 'That was nice,' she says.

'What was?'

'The call I just had.'

'Oh, from Aunty Susan?'

'No, it wasn't Susan, it was a friend of yours. She can't make the wedding today but was phoning to say good luck to you. She asked whether you got back OK last night and whether you had fun on the hen weekend.'

'Which friend was that? Everyone I invited to the wedding can come.'

'Oh, I don't know. I forgot to check. She was asking who was on the hen weekend and whether you had a good time.'

'How odd.'

CHAPTER 23

Once my makeup has been finished, Jackie steps back in to make sure my hair is perfect. They're like a tag team. Then I'm helped into my dress before Janine does a bit more fussing with the makeup, then more hair teasing, as Jackie fixes the veil in place.

'Oh darling, you look wonderful,' says mum.

She stands next to me in her lovely navy outfit which matches the bridesmaids' dresses so perfectly. Juan comes to join us.

'They've just landed. The bridesmaids are on their way,' he says.

'Oh thank goodness. Oh, I'm so pleased. Everything is going to be perfect.'

'Don't cry,' says mum. 'You don't want to smudge your make up.'

'Oh hell!' shouts Juan.

'What's the matter?' asks mum. 'Nothing. No. Nothing at all.'

'There must be something wrong.'

'No, no…as you were. Nothing to worry anyone.'

I look at Juan. He's ashen-faced, despite the heavy application of bronzer that he persuaded Janine to give him.

'What's the matter?'

'Oh Mary, It's just this...'

He hands me his iPad.

DRUNK HEN PARTY arrested after flashing at police while dressed as nuns.

Mail Online EXCLUSIVE by Melodie Breakspeare

SIX BRITS on a wild and drunken hen night in Crete spent a night in police cells after cops caught them staggering through the streets wearing nuns' outfits while behaving in a disgraceful and offensive manner. The alcohol-fuelled women had been dancing, flirting, and flashing their bottoms at onlookers, including the local police, while dressed in nuns' habits.

A FOREIGN OFFICE spokeswoman said the formal change against the middle-aged women was: 'causing a scandal by provocative acts and misrepresenting a uniform.'

THE TOURISTS, ranging in ages from 40 to 'about 60', were led into the courtroom on Monday morning after being allowed to return to their hotel the previous evening to change into 'non-offensive' clothing.

. . .

They had spent a night in police custody after being arrested in the early hours of Sunday morning at Hotel Cristina. The arrest came after a night of partying got out of hand.

'They were completely outrageous; flashing at everyone and being really rude while wearing religious clothing,' said a member of the hotel staff.

The unemployed women entered the courtroom with the assistance of the police and court officials.

It was understood charges were dropped against the group, but they were warned about their offensive behaviour.

Mail Online has approached Mary Brown, the leader of the hen party, and asked for comment. It is believed that Brown returned home on a flight last night, while other members of the group remain in Crete and will miss the wedding.'

'Oh my God.'

'I know. It's completely outrageous,' says Juan. 'Middle-aged women? What? None of us are even approaching middle-aged. This is a travesty. Can we sue?'

'But how do they know all this? How the hell do they know that we came back last night and the rest of the girls didn't? I don't understand. What's the journalist's name again?'

'It's Melodie Breakspeare,' says Juan.

'Melodie?' says mum. 'Did you say that someone called Melodie has written about you in the Mail?'

'Yes. She's written about the hen weekend. There's nothing to worry about at all, we just don't know where she got all her information.

'Oh right,' says mum.

I look around the room at all the faces, none of them quite knows what's going on, but they have an inkling that there's something in the paper about our hen weekend. I see nothing but astonishment that our weekend has found its way into the Daily Mail. Then I look at mum's face…it's the colour of freshly chopped beetroot.

OK. I think we know where the problem lies.

Mum's face reminds me of those videos you see of dogs misbehaving. The owner of the dogs stands there, asking which of them broke the toilet, and the camera pans slowly from one dog to the next as they all look entirely innocent. Then, at the end of the line, a dog with a toilet seat around his neck looks exceptionally sheepish.

'Mum!' I say.

'What?'

'Why have you gone scarlet?'

'It's hot in here.'

'No, it isn't. Did you talk to the Daily Mail?'

'Well, I hope I haven't. But I've remembered now. The woman I spoke to – the one who said she was your friend – Melodie Breakspeare. I thought she was someone coming to the wedding. She asked me whether you were back, and I told her you were. I said you'd arrived back safely last night. The person then asked if you were OK, and I said yes, but the bridesmaids weren't back yet. I had no idea who she was, love. Then she asked about your arrest in Crete, and I thought it was a joke. You weren't arrested in Crete, were you?

'Oh, God.'

'Why did she say you were arrested?'

'Oh mum, it was nothing. Just a mistake by the Greek police.'

'So, you were arrested?'

'Kind of.'

'Honestly, it was nothing,' says Juan. 'Just a silly mix-up and the papers think it sounds like a good story. Please don't worry.'

'Oh well. If you're sure.'

'Yes, it will all blow over. Just don't speak to anyone who calls you. Switch your phone off, mum. I'm surprised you've got it on. It's never on when I call you.'

'Well I made sure I charged it up last night and switched it on because there'll be lots happening today...I need to make sure people can get hold of me.'

'Oh, I love you, mum,' I say, giving her a huge hug. 'Don't worry about a thing. Everything's going to be just fine. Now, let's go and make sure dad's ready, and let's see where these bridesmaids are.'

I glance at Juan and see the look of nervousness on his face.

'No one will see it; it's just Mail Online. No one reads that.'

I appreciate the sentiment of his words, but the truth is that everyone reads Mail Online; they read it all around the world.

CHAPTER 24

'You look stunning, sweetheart,' says dad as we sit in the car on the way to the palace. 'Really lovely.'

'Thank you,' I say, feeling a warmth snake through my stomach. 'I'm so excited to be marrying Ted.'

'Good, so you should be. You two are perfect together.'

'Are you pleased, dad?'

'Oh blimey, yes. He's a great guy. Really great. And way better than any of those boyfriends you brought back before him. Good lord, where did you find those men?'

'They weren't all so bad. Stop exaggerating.'

'One of them had earrings all the way up his ear and only half a beard.'

'Yeah, OK. He might have been a mistake.'

'And what about the guy who worked at the fun fair? He was a rogue.'

'Yeah, that might be a fair comment.'

'And the hairdresser you dated. Well, if he wasn't gay, I'm a banana.'

'OK, dad. Perhaps you have a point. Good job I found my Ted.'

'An excellent job. I'm sure you're going to make each other very happy.'

'You know, when we were on the hen weekend, I met this guy who asked me how I knew Ted was 'the one.' It was hard to explain, so I just said I knew. I haven't got one doubt. Were you like that with mum?'

'I was exactly like that. I still am. I remember your mother walking down the aisle looking beautiful, like you do now, and thinking that I couldn't love anyone any more than I loved her at that minute.'

'Ahh, that's lovely, dad.'

'No, but I was wrong.'

'What do you mean, you were wrong?'

'I mean that it turned out I could love her more than I did that minute. I love her more every day. I look at her and feel like the luckiest man alive. Oh, I know she's not all beautiful and perfect like on our wedding day. But the grey hairs and the wrinkles don't matter. They've got nothing to do with love; love is inside you. Love is knowing that someone always wants the best for you; it's knowing that you'd rather break your legs than have a hair on her head hurt. I think you and Ted will be like that, love. I see so much of your mum in you.'

'I'm glad about that. I've got lots of you in me too.'

'I know, love. Sorry about that!'

JUAN AND MUM have waited at the house to let the bridesmaids in when they return from Crete. They will follow on as soon as they can. For now, though, it's just dad and me.

I step out of the car when I arrive at the venue, assisted by

Steve, one of Ted's friends. Steve's lovely. Ted should have made him the best man instead of that muppet, Mike.

Steve even stays to help me straighten my skirts in the absence of bridesmaids.

'Does my hair look OK?' I ask dad.

'Oh blimey – it looks lovely to me, sweetheart, but I'm a bit out of my comfort zone. Not an expert on women's hair.'

'I think it looks amazing,' says Steve. 'You look beautiful. Mary. Really beautiful.'

A car pulls up behind us, and Juan jumps out and runs round to let my mum out. He walks with her to join us.

'Can I have the honour of escorting you inside, Mrs. Brown?' says Steve to my mum.

'Oh, you are kind. Thank you. Are you OK if I go in, Mary? Is there anything you need?'

'I'm fine. Thanks for everything, mum. You're a star.'

It leaves just dad, Juan, and me, hovering by the door.

'Apparently, I have to give them a sign when you're ready to go,' says Juan. 'Do you want to hang on for the bridesmaids or go without them?'

'Let's wait,' I say. 'I need my team around me.'

'Excellent,' says Juan, as dad gives me a hug.

To be fair to the girls, they quickly get to us. They must have got changed in about five minutes. They pile out of the car and come running towards me at break-neck speed.

'You look amazing. Oh my God, your hair is stunning. I love your make-up…' The compliments come tumbling out.

'I don't think we should keep him waiting anymore,' says Juan. 'I'm going to give the sign.'

The music strikes up, the girls align themselves, and down the makeshift aisle, we walk. The place looks lovely. Mum and aunty Susan have excelled themselves.

As I walk through my friends and family, I hear the sound of crying and a lady's voice wailing. I know that'll be mum, bless her. She loves Ted almost as much as I do; she obviously can't contain her emotions.

But then I hear the wailing and crying again and realise it's coming from just behind me. It's Juan, in floods of tears.

I glance around and smile, but he doesn't notice me. He's such a soppy little thing. I do love him.

Then, I see Ted.

Standing there.

Waiting for me.

He looks lovely.

His suit is perfect, his hair looks like it's been cut this morning, and he's freshly shaven. But the main thing I notice is his lovely, big smile. He steps forward to take me from my dad and tells me how beautiful I look.

'Let's get married,' he says.

The service itself is short. That's what we asked for. A brief but warm and friendly service and exchange of rings. That's all we need.

When the words 'you may kiss the bride' come, I'm well and truly in tears. Ted kisses them away, then kisses me on the lips. We hold out our hands so our rings touch.

'Forever,' he says.

'Forever.'

THERE'S a lot to do on a wedding day, isn't there? I'm dying to be left alone with Ted for just a few minutes, but no sooner have we said *I do* than everyone wants to talk to us and hug us. They are rushing around us. Mum is smoothing down my hair, and Juan is offering me the lipstick Janine told me to reapply through the day.

'Don't worry, it's not dark plum,' he says as I apply the light peach colour.

There are photographs and more mingling and talking to

everyone, then it's time to go inside for the wedding breakfast and the speeches. I've asked Charlie to make a speech for me. I know it's not usual for the bride's friend to stand up, but I think it will make the whole thing much more balanced if we have a female voice in there,

Dad is the first speech giver. He's remarkably good at making speeches. You wouldn't think it if you spent time with him socially, he's not great at small talk and isn't overly keen on talking to strangers, but he thrives when you put him on a stage. Perhaps he should have been an actor, a tv presenter, or something. He seems to flourish when he's presenting to people in a way that he doesn't when he's chatting socially.

He tells everyone about the many times I'd go out partying when I was younger, and he'd have to wait for me outside. He tells them about when he instructed me to be outside the nightclub at midnight, and I wasn't, so he went in his painting overalls to find me. Everyone laughed uproariously. Then he had a more serious moment when he said how much he liked Ted and how glad he was to welcome him to the family.

My dad's speech was hilarious, and I loved it. He took the mickey out of me without mocking or making me feel bad. I think that's quite an art. I've seen many speeches that derive all their humour from knocking the bride and the bridesmaids.

Next, it's time for Charlie to speak. Now, this is where I'm definitely going to be mocked.

Hello ladies and gentlemen; I know most of you here today. My name is Charlie, and this is the part of the proceedings known as 'tribute to the bride' but which I like to call REVENGE.

I met Mary around 15 years ago, and one of the first things we did when we became firm friends was to do some personal training

sessions together. Mary had been a gymnast, so I knew she was competitive, but I never realised how competitive until we got going.

We contacted this lovely Spanish lady who came round to my house and put us both through our paces in the nearby parks and on the steps of Hampton Court Palace, where we had to run up and down and generally be beaten up by her. But before we started, she suggested that we do some fitness tests so she could assess what level we were at and have a marker to look back on to gauge our improvements.

So we started with press-ups, and I assumed the knee press-up position and prepared to do a press-up. About halfway through my first one, I heard off, ooofff, ooofff from beside me. I looked over, and Mary was in the proper press-up position going up and down like mad as if she was trying to get into the paras or the marines.

When the instructor read the scores, it was: Charlie 8: Mary 643.

It was the same for sit-ups ups.

Mary has been a very kind and caring friend to me: incredibly loyal and great fun, and my life has been happier for her being in it, but she does have her moments. And sometimes you can't quite believe what she's said. I'll give you a few examples... We had lunch in the pub nearby, and the waiter walked out with a massive plate of food on a tray. There were roast potatoes, vegetables, and a colossal piece of meat. It looked delicious. Mary looked over at the two men receiving it and shouted: 'If you need a hand with that, just shout. At that point, she realised one of the guys only had one hand. Well done, Mary.

EVERYONE ROARS with laughter as Charlie recounts all the silly things I've done over the years. She describes the time I ironed my skirt in the morning, then rushed out to get the bus, leaving it lying on the ironing board. She describes the time I met this great guy at a party and was chatting away to him, only for Juan to come along and tell me I was talking to the mirror.

Mary, you are an absolute angel. You are one of the best people I know - funny, bright, clever, and kind. Ted, you are the luckiest man in the world. I wish you every happiness imaginable, and I'm so pleased, honoured, and delighted to be in your lives.

It's a brilliant speech, and everyone stands up and cheers raucously. The clapping continues for ages until Mike rises to his feet and coughs into the microphone.

'My turn,' he says. 'Brace yourselves.'

CHAPTER 25

Mike looks around at his audience and smiles.

It's hard to know where to start, really. I met Ted at school, and we became good friends straight away. We played rugby together, and both loved it. We played at a decent level and travelled all over the place for matches and tournaments. We had the best time.

But then, one day, Ted sustained a severe rugby injury while trying to balance out the scrum. His injury required surgery and a long time of recuperation. After that, he never played rugby again.

I need to explain that he fought so hard to keep that scrum up to prevent me from getting hurt. I probably haven't told him how much this means to me over the years. This great lump of a man put his body on the line to save mine, and I'll never forget that. He's the best of men. The very best.

. . .

'THAT'S LOVELY,' I say to Ted. 'He's right, though. You're the best person ever.'

AND THE THING IS – I've always felt like I owed Ted for what he did. But owed him in a way that I would never be able to pay back. You can never pay someone back when they save you from injury. But I thought I'd try by researching a subject he might be interested in. You see, research is relatively easy for me because I'm in the police, so I get access to all sorts of juicy information. So I thought I might tell you some particularly juicy stuff today. What do you think?'

'YES!' we all chorus. The hens and I shout louder than most: 'Tell us everything, Mike.'

Ted stays silent, save a whisper to me:

'Oh blimey, what on earth is he going to say?'

THEN LET ME BEGIN... The tradition at weddings is for the best man to give a speech on the assumption that the groom is the worse behaved of the two people marrying and has more to hide, providing lots of ammunition for the best man. Well, not in this case. Ladies and gentlemen, you will be thrilled to hear that I found out what went on when the girls went on their hen weekend, and it's quite an eye-opener.

'YAY!!!!' everyone shouts. 'Come on, Mike, tell us what they got up to.'

I look over at the hens, who sit in silence, confused and worried.

. . .

You've heard of four weddings and a funeral. This is five bridesmaids and a police cell. Yep, I have discovered that our bride and her bridesmaids were arrested in Crete and thrown into a police cell overnight. That's why they were so late back.

I look at Ted, but he's not looking at me; he's staring at Mike, his jaw clenched in anger.

I thought it was odd that they were so delayed, and I didn't trust their excuse that the flight was full. Really, girls? Every flight, all day? So, I phoned up and asked whether I could book a ticket. Guess what, there were loads of seats on the plane.

That's when I knew something was amiss.

Then, Mary arrived last night, clutching a picture of herself in a nun's habit. I've been sent abroad to stag parties who get themselves arrested for dressing as nuns. Crete is a religious country. I put two and two together and knew what had happened. I called the police in Crete and was told all about it. Six hens in Crete flashing their bottoms while dressed as nuns were locked in a police cell overnight. It took a lawyer and the British consulate in Crete to get them out of it. They were in court yesterday. That's why they were late back. And, another thing...'

'Thanks, Mike. That's lovely. You can sit down now,' says Ted

'But I've got loads more to say. I was going to tell them about the time you did sumo wrestling and fell through the window. I haven't told any of the fun stuff yet.'

'Might have been good if you'd started with that. OK, ladies and gentlemen. That's where we wrap up the speeches.

I hope you enjoy your meals and the dancing and drinking to follow.'

I look over at Mike, still standing there, pint in hand, stomach hanging over his trousers. Everyone else is staring at me, open-mouthed at what they've heard. Mum looks confused, and Dad seems embarrassed. I don't know whether I should say something, stay seated or feign a heart attack.

But then Ted starts talking again:

'I'd like to add a few things after Mike's speech. But, first, I must comment on what a colourful imagination he has. I never realised. But then, he has been in the police all his adult life, so perhaps exaggeration comes more naturally to him than it does to the rest of us.

'The truth is that I'm very proud to be married to a woman who knows how to have fun. I'm delighted that my beautiful bride is a bundle of unpredictability and joy. I'm pleased they had an enormously fun weekend and managed to get themselves into such an unholy mess but still got back safely.

'Mary Brown, you have chaos in your veins and beauty in your soul. I love you now, and I will love you forever.'

Oh God, how did I meet someone so wonderful? There's a giant rush as all the hens run to our table to hug and kiss Ted. He's mobbed while Mike sits there with his arms folded.

'I'm sorry I didn't tell you. I didn't want you to worry. I was going to run through the whole thing and tell you all about it after the wedding,' I say, while the hens cling to Ted and ask him whether he has any brothers or male cousins he could introduce them to.

'In the future, just tell me, then I won't have to read about it in the Daily Mail.'

'You read that?'

'Of course I did.'

'Well, I suppose it's better than Mike's speech being a complete surprise to you. You must have been so shocked when you saw it. I'm really sorry I didn't tell you.'

'I kind of thought something was up. I wasn't expecting you to end up in a police cell, but I knew something wasn't right. Then I saw the article.'

'Do you know how the Daily Mail got all that information?'

'I assumed they got it from journalists in Crete.'

'Yeah, well, they got some of it from mum. They rang her pretending to be a friend of mine and asked all about the hen weekend.'

'Blimey,' he says. Then he goes quiet for a moment. 'Did you really spend a night in a police cell?'

'Yep.'

'How was it?'

'It was completely terrifying and very uncomfortable.'

'I hope you're going to behave yourself on your honeymoon.'

'I'll try,' I say.

'So, do you want to know where we're going?'

'Oh, yes, please. I'm dying to know.'

'We're off to St Lucia,' he says with a flourish.

'Oh My God. That's amazing. Really amazing.'

'And we're off on Thursday, so we can relax tomorrow before we leave for two weeks of lazing around on beautiful white beaches in the sunshine.'

'Oh, it sounds wonderful,'

He kisses me gently on the lips.

'It's time for me to get this beautiful lady home,' he says, standing up and helping me to my feet. 'You all be careful and try not to get yourself arrested while we're on honeymoon, won't you.'

'We'll try. No guarantees, though,' says Juan. 'You know how it is.'

'I know how it is,' says Ted, shaking hands with Juan and hugging all the girls. 'We'll see you in two weeks,'

Everyone rushes out after us as we leave and walk along the river. They throw tiny blossom petals which flutter down beside us. I'm with the man of my dreams, who has stood by me through all the madness, crazy times, and unpredictability. So many things have happened over the years that made me worry I'd lose him. Not least, the hen weekend that shall never be mentioned. But that's all behind us now as we walk through the shower of flowers.

'I've never been so happy,' I say to him.

'Me neither, angel. Me neither.'

'I promise to tell you everything that happened in Crete. But you mustn't tell anyone.'

'OK,' he says.

'I mean it. We made a promise: Don't Mention The Hen Weekend.'

THIS IS the latest in the series of Mary Brown books. To read others in the series, see Bernice Bloom Books on Amazon. This is the link: https://amzn.to/3zUs7J3

TO READ about Mary and Ted's adventures on honeymoon in St Lucia, why not join Bernice's newsletter? You will hear all about the writing of the book and be the first to know when the book goes on sale. To sign up for the newsletter go to my website: www.bernicebloom.com and a box should pop up.

Any problems, just email me on: bernicenovelist@gmail.com

Printed in Great Britain
by Amazon

44864470R00111